Hotel Chiller

by

JANE VESPE

AuthorHouse™
1663 Liberty Drive
Bloomington, IN 47403
www.authorhouse.com
Phone: 1 (800) 839-8640

Published by AuthorHouse 06/04/2019

ISBN: 978-1-7283-0309-3 (sc)
ISBN: 978-1-7283-0308-6 (e)

Print information available on the last page.

authorHOUSE®

About The Book

This book is about a married couple Richard and Leena Fine.

Richard Fine is a self -made millionaire. Richard Fine is owner of Hotel Chiller in Los Angeles California and runs one of the biggest chain of hotels in the State of California. Mr. Fine is retired and part-time from his job for about a year. He wanted to spend more time writing books. He always dreamed of writing book about glamourous actresses that he met in Hollywood California and in Los Angeles. Many of whom, who spent their time at Hotel Chiller.

Leena Fine is a manager of a clothing store at Hotel Chiller and actress. Mrs. Fine is also, a freelance journalist and writer. She has written several cookbooks on healthy eating. She also stared in a famous Soap Opera Riker's Hospital.

Richard was always fascinated with glamourous women. This inspired him to go to college for four years where he obtained a Master's Degree in English. During his studies, Richard Fine travelled the world.

For years, Richard Fine took photos from events that he attended in Europe and California. He also got his inspiration for writing when his wife Leena appeared on the television show Riker's Hospital back in the eighties. When Richard travelled the world with his gorgeous wife Leena, he kept a very large photo collection of glamourous ladies and celebrities. He saved them until he was ready to write.

Anyone who knows the Fines can tell that these two millionaires love travelling around the world. They are not your average everyday couple. Wherever they go, excitement is in the air. They are always up for a challenge. You never know what is going to happen at any event. Another interesting thing about them is that they seem to find murder or trouble wherever they go, whether it's on vacation or book signing events. Or, because they're trying to help bail out a friend. Murder and trouble are their hobby, especially when they met.

However, as busy as they are, they still find lots of time for love and snuggles in between and keep their marriage full of love.

In this story, Richard Fine finally publishes his first book "I Loved Her In The Eighties, " and meets his fans for the very first time. He and his wife Leena are also trying to solve the disappearance of their daughter. Richard and Leena Fine meet up with many fans.

In this story Richard first attending his first book signing event and speaks out on his new book, "I Loved Her in The Eighties."

He introduces his actresses Maria St. John who he has met in the eighties. Then, he goes and speaks about the nighties and how he photographed gorgeous actors and actresses. This Including Rachael Goldstein from the picture "Civil Liberties," and Jim Rod who appeared in "Ben Franklin, Long Ago."

One fan Sara Novella travelled to his events and became suspicious of someone stalking the author Richard Fine. This stalker also becomes obsessed with his wife Leena Fine.

Sara a dedicated fan, becomes suspicious at his first book signing event and even more suspicious at the Graveyard Theater event in New Jersey. Sara witnesses the stalker trying to attempt to hurt Mr. Fine while waiting on line. Sara runs to security and tries to stop him. Sara does get questioned by Mr. Fine right before she is threatened and clams up in the photo room, trying to hide information because she's scared. If a judge were to find out Sara was in danger, she could be put into custody for her disability.

In a years' time, Richard becomes an aspiring writer who gets more than he bargains for when his favorite best-selling book "I Loved Her In The Eighties," reaches a stalker who finally threatens Richard and his wife. The stalker also scares three thousand people including his wife, at one of his books signing event in Parsippany, New Jersey.

Chapter One

The Revue

The Revue Mr. Fine's private jet is coming in for a landing. Mr. Fine is sitting in his swivel chair and he is coming in for a landing for the first time and attending some autograph book signing events in New York. Mr. Fine flew to Long Island, New York to attend his first book signing event at the Revue in Madison, New York. He flew in his business lier jet. Even though Mr. Fine is great pilot and knows all about jets.He decided to sit out and hire a pilot to fly him to New York. With the utmost most comfort, Mr. Fine knew his week would be long and he would be tired.

As is plane was coming in for a landing he sat back in his brown recliner that swiveled around, and had his legs crossed smirking, hoping his wife Leena will be waiting at home for his call when his plane lands. When his plane landed, he sat back in his swivel recliner in his fancy jet for about an hour after landing before gathering his stuff and grabbing his personal items. He picked up his cell phone and called Leena.

Mr. Fine: "I landed darling." Did you pack my tie or did the dogs take it? (He asked)?

Mrs. Fine: I packed an extra tie. I packed two for you honey in case the dogs decided to chew on them. One tie is in a bag and I hid it on him, exclaimed Mrs. Fine!

Mr. Fine: "That's what I love about you darling!" You always know what to do and how to handle everything. I will call you later this evening. I will double check my clothes. I am leaving now for a business meeting with my publisher and then on my way to the Revue in Madison, N.Y.

Mrs. Fine: I love you too darling and she blew kisses over the phone as he blew kisses back to her.

Mr. Fine hung up the phone and heated a meal up in the microwave. He looked through his suitcase and found the dog took one tie. He didn't have much time. He had another brandy in his cabin before leaving and walking through the airport terminal, heading towards his hotel. The chauffeur was outside the front of the airport and he was wearing a limousine-style cloak. He opened the side door for Mr. Fine as he got in the limo. Mr. Fine met up with Marie St. John, in whom he wrote about in his book "I Loved Her in The Eighties." Mr. Fine got out of his stretch limousine with actress from the eighties spy movie Bonding is a Crime: Marie St. John. She is also co producer and writer of Riker's Hospital.

Mr. Fine and Marie St. John were getting ready to go to the Revue in Madison New York, to greet his fans for the first time. Behind Mr. Fine was his publicist Deb Rivera. Mr. Fine went to the Revue coat room real fast to get changed. He was cracking jokes about his dogs eating his tie. He didn't like the other tie that was packed. The lovely greeter told Mr. Fine they have extra ties and clothing in the coat room. She told Mr. Fine there's also a changing room in the back. Mr. Fine thanked the girl and said he just needs to change his shirt. When Mr. Fine suspected the dog had his blue necktie, he packed along a black turtleneck top real fast as a backup because he was running out of time. Mr. Fine went inside real fast to get changed and then came outside to take photos with fans.

Mr. Fine was so excited to be speaking on his new book at the Revue in Madison, New York. Fans all around the world came to the Revue to listen to Richard Fine speak on Wednesday, November 15, 2016. Sara Novella, her cousin Jean Novella, and Jean's brother Robert Novella travelled for hours to see Richard Fine speak at this event. They were all fans going into the Revue to listen to this celebrity speak on Wednesday, November 15, 2016 at 5:30 pm.

Outside the Book Revue in Madison, New York, fans waited and took pictures. There they posed by the window and posed for pictures with Richard Fine. Richard Fine looked debonair standing outside the Revue.

He is six feet tall, dark silver hair with brown streaks. He has blue eyes and sophisticated to look at. He looked so handsome in his black turtleneck. While taking photos, one girl had his head on his shoulder, while the other girl laid her chin and stared at him. Sara was disappointed in the beginning because she didn't get her picture with Richard Fine. Then another was snapping a picture. Sara wandered what cologne he had on. He must have smelled good for the girls to be all over him. Sara mumbled to Jean, let's play the guessing game of what cologne he is wearing. But they didn't want to look obnoxious just yet. It was their first time meeting a famous author. They decided to go back inside, act normal, and give Mr. Fine his space. They knew their time with photos was coming. They were grateful just to be among the fans and a part of the evening's audience.

Fans are all outside taking pictures with Mr. Fine. Sara, Jean and Robert went back inside to grab seats. The best thing about this was Sara, Jean and Robert were able to get front and second row seats. The seating was very comfortable and facing the smoked wing-style podium. Chairs were shaped like a horseshoe facing the podium. This room went from empty to packed by 6:30 pm. Fans are waiting patiently and taking pictures.

Robert decided to take photos of Sara in a black top and green pants. Jean was in a green top and denim pants sitting behind Sara. Fans waited patiently as Mr. Fine was finishing up photos outside. People started getting quiet as the announcer was telling them Mr. Fine is on his way in.

Finally, the speaker announces Mr. Fine as a new author with his bestselling book, "I Loved Her in The Eighties." Mr. Fine revisits celebrity hangouts in the eighties which defined the times in his latest book. Finally, the speaker announces could you please welcome our new author Richard Fine.

Everyone stood up and fans from all over the world clapped for several minutes. They continued to applaud and stand. When Mr. Fine walked out to the podium, he stared directly at the audience and started waving to all. As his hand rose in the air, he smiled so handsomely at the audience walking to the podium.

Sara notice one suspicious guy acting kind of funny but ignored him and continued to clap for Mr. Fine. This guy was bald and about 5'5 and somewhat thin. He had white hair and one eye looked kind of weird and lazy, which made Sara nervous.

Mr. Fine: Mr. Fine stepped out and gave the speaker a huge huge hug and big whopping kiss after he shuck hands with her at the podium. When He reached the center of the podium, he stood there for several minutes starring overwhelmed at the audience. He was so humbled and embraced the audience by opening his arms up and thanking all of them for coming. He thanked everyone several times. He kept saying Wow! How great this is! Mr. Fine first thanked his fans: "Wow" How Great Thou Art" and Great it is to be in such company of wonderful readers and enthusiastic fans who came out to see me tonight. I have been very blessed!

I want to share my blessing with everyone. It's so nice of you to come out and greet me for the first time. I am so flattered to see such a great audience and decided that after my lecture I will take several questions from the audience and answer them as appropriately as I can.

I was always interested in writing exclaimed Mr. Fine. I watched my wife for years write on extremely popular people and interview celebrities. She took photos and I took photos. I saved my photos in a collection until I decided to partly retire from Hotel Chiller. After I retired, I decided to go to college and get my Masters in writing. This was the one thing I was lacking, was having degree in life. I finally decided to go for it while I am still living on this earth. I travelled around the world prior and saved photos of prominent people I met on my journeys. I said one day I will publish this information in a book and share it with others.

Tonight, I stand here and have achieved my goals in doing that. (The audience applauded).

Mr. Fine: (First introduces his book "I Loved Her in The Eighties,") as a book dedicated to the celebrities who brought television to its peak and reached many throughout our world. This was considered the Great Time in Television. I dedicated my book to my glamorous wife Leena Fine. I also dedicated my book to my daughter who was missing. She disappeared, Richard said.

We are still praying for her safe return home. She was our daughter he exclaimed! She also cooked, cleaned and was our best friend. We used to go on many day trips in our yellow Mercedes Bends. We used to drive to Napa Valley, California. We would stop at the winery tour and then take a cruise into San Francisco. We always did a family outing there. Our daughter's name was Lynn Marie Fine. She also worked at Hotel Chiller. One of my favorite things to do with her was picnic in the grassy parks of Sacramento, California.

Then he mentioned their dogs Scotch and Whisky. He mentioned how they found them. Lynn found them when she was fifteen and found them drinking by the whiskey bottle. This happened on coming home from one trip from Napa Valley and we saw Whisky licking his paw and gnawing at his paw and licking a whiskey bottle. He holds up a picture of Whisky and Scotch. This is a picture of Whisky and Scotch. They look so innocent but they're not. (audience laughs). Mrs. Fine is always dressing them up and putting costumes on them for laughs. (audience laughs).

Mrs. Fine is always finding them messing around with stuff, especially my clothes and taking pictures. Scotch was playing with the cork.

Richard said, I know some of you saw me outside and saw that Maria St. John was holding my clothes. I had to change because Whisky stole my tie and probably is eating it right now. My wife packed an extra one, but I decided to wear the turtleneck instead. Richard cracked a joke. He said at least he didn't eat my speech, then he'd be in the doghouse!

The audience laughed as they cheered him on. Clapping went on for several minutes. I can't wait to find his stash, and get my tie back. That's because my wife ran out of chips, so they ate my tie. (audience laughs). I have a picture somewhere with them eating chips. (He pulled it out and show the audience). (The audience laughs).

Fans were just fascinated as they titled their head and began listening to him speak about the first three chapters of his book. "I Loved Her in The Eighties."

Mr. Fine first speaks out in chapter one on Maria St. John, was extremely glamorous and invited me on the set of "Bonding Is A Crime," because directors wanted to use different rooms from his hotel as their lab source in the movie where chemicals were made for their explosions.

I asked if my wife and I could visit the set and collect photos while they were filming, and director Thomas Spiels said of course, since it was my hotel they were using. This was the start of meeting many celebrities.

In the meantime, I helped our police department solve many crimes and attended many events outside of being a hotel owner. Mr. Fine spoke about the first three chapters in his book. He described the first chapter what it was like attending celebrity events with Mrs. Fine. He said he went to many musicals where celebrities like Marie St. John attended as well. Mr. Fine then goes into chapter two of his book and described what it was like working with Rachael Goldstein. He describes how big of a fan his daughter was of her show and adored her role in Civil Liberties Film. Lynn met Rachael Goldstein and a food festival in San Francisco California where they took classes in evening one year. Lynn cooked a dish for us Mr. Fine said. It was delicious. I forgot what the name of it was.

Lynn was with me for many years. She was the rock of our home. Lynn did whatever we asked of her. Lynn was there for us. Whether we took children in, Lynn knew how to treat them and take care of them. Lynn always helped in tough times and pitched in when Mrs. Fine and I were in a jam. She always took care of our dogs when we went away and made sure they were well fed.

She was amazing, she just knew what to do with anything that was handed to her. She never got jealous if we took in kids. She always wanted to help. Even when times were tough in the Hotel. "How can I help Dad?" she would say. How? Lynn

was twenty-five years old. She had reddish medium hair and gray eyes. Guys use to love her in the hotel.

I can remember one time when Lynn helped us out when our home was ransacked. Someone was trying to attempt to rob the house. Someone came in and tried to rob our home while we were away at the ranch. I came home because I injured my back and came home early to find my house in shambles and Lynn took care of everything. The house was almost cleaned up by the time Leena and I returned. I was so proud of her. She was brave for coming home from the hotel and finding our house robbed. She called the police, she filled out the report and made sure the two dogs were safe. She had the kitchen cleaned up and was working on cleaning the living room. I was so impressed that I treated Lynn to a vacation to Hawaii for two weeks and allowed her to miss school. She was excited. (the audience chuckled).

She was graduating anyway, and I decided to give her an early graduation gift. I was so amazed at the way she uses to pick up on my instincts whenever we tried to help police solve crimes. For some reason, she just knew what to do. I'm hoping for her safe return home. I have a few minutes to finish up.

In closing, I just want to add that Jim Rod as another great actor to meet and he played Ben Franklin. Many filmmakers used our hotel for layout plans whenever there were explosions or labs in their films. Or, when stars had to film getaways, my hotel was used. There were always cameras. Our hotel always had a new film each week and still do. Directors from all over the world stop in and want to observe Hotel Chiller, which had two large theaters inside.

It had a Gotham Look for movies and films. It has great shops. One which my wife manages. If you ever look at the film credits to some of the movies you would see the name Hotel Chiller and a picture of some of the rooms where they filmed. My hotel is listed in the credit section of films. There were also several rooms where celebrities could sign autographs, three restaurants and a nice bar. Hotel Chiller is a wonderful hotel to stay at and you will always find a celebrity. It has become a hang out joint for celebrities. (audience laughs).

In closing, I wanted to add Lynn was twenty-five years old as I said before (he holds up a picture) she has gray eyes and is 5'5. She's on the chunky side and she has a scar on her left arm. She fell off a bike when she was a kid when riding for the first time.

I will take several questions from the audience and then I will be signing books in the other room. Many fans raised their hands.

Chapter 2

Questions and Answers with Mr. Fine At the Revue

Fan One: Mr. Fine did you ever invite any celebrities to your home and have parties at your house?

Mr. Fine: Yes, one celebrity was Jim Rod. He was filming at Christmas time and when Hotel Chiller became a part of his picture, I decided to invite him to my holiday party.

Fan Two: Was Rachael Goldstein ever at your house?

Mr. Fine: As a matter of speaking yes but not at Christmas time. Lynn and Rachael teamed up for a food festival cooking contest for the best chili dish. Lynn made the best chili. Rachael loved Lynn's chili. They decided to team up and compete in a chili contest. There were three prizes. First prize, was an appearance on a cooking show. Second prize, was for $5,000 in cash. Third prize, was their recipe printed in a magazine. Rachael and Lynn won third prize. Who would a thought a teenager with a celebrity could win a cooking contest?

Fan Three: Mr. Fine is there a Hollywood celebrity you wished to write on and maybe put it in your next book.

Mr. Fine: Yes, Gerard Rico from the film Science Bums, which is a comedy. Gerard and I became acquainted. I added him at the end of this chapter but didn't fully write everything that should be said. He was another celebrity too that was invited to my house during the holidays.

Fan Four: Mr. Fine did they ever find out what happened to Lynn and implicate anyone?

Sara: Sara shuck her head and starred at Jean and Robert) Really, she said? And Mr. Fine turned to look at Sara and smiled. (he cracked up when Sara opened her mouth).

Mr. Fine: Mr. Fine hesitated and said Lynn disappeared that's all I know.

Robert: Turned to Sara and said…

Robert: Shush! Keep it low!

Sara: He's a moron . .. she whispered.

Robert: Yeah, I'm sure Mr. Fine knows that, but he can handle him. Remember he works with police and solves crimes remember?

Sara: Yeah alright but still. He's still a hole Mr. Fine giggled and smirked at Sara. Robert shuck his head and laughed as well.

Fan Five: Mr. Fine are you planning on writing anymore books?

Mr. Fine: Yes, I am I have quite a few celebrities to introduce and hopefully in a two years' time I will have another book out.

Fan Six: Mr. Fine, will you be doing anymore book signing events?

Mr. Fine: Yes, I will I will be In LC in NYC with actress Lisa Smith tomorrow evening. Mr. Fine thanked everyone for coming. I will be heading towards the autograph signing room where I will be signing autographs and chatting with you. I hope to see you all there. Thank you so much for coming. Mr. Fine turned left and headed towards the autograph signing room.

Chapter 3

Autographs with Mr. Fine

The first fan came forward to get her booked signed Her name was Krissy Shaw. Krissy was in front of Sara. Sara was second in line. The idiot that was making comments before was behind Sara. He continued to make threatening comments. He was escorted out of the line into the other room to cool off. He was told by the security guard that if he didn't cool it, they will call a cop on him and have him arrested.

Mr. Fine: Where are you from Mr. Fine asked?

Krissy: I'm from Long Island said Krissy. My name is Krissy Shaw. I'm a big fan of television shows from the eighties. I'm glad you wrote a book on them. Your photos of celebrities are fantastic. Such great stories in each chapter. I truly enjoyed your book. I hope you write on many more celebrities from the eighties and attend more book signing events. It's such a shame your beautiful wife Leena couldn't make it.

Mr. Fine: (so humbled as he put both hands over Krissy's hand). Thank you so much. I truly appreciate those words and thank you so much for coming out for the first time. It's such a wonderful pleasure to meet you.

Krissy: Could you please sign my book to Krissy love Richard Fine??

Mr. Fine: Sure, I can. I will be more than happy to do that.

Krissy: Thank you. I hope you do more book signing events.

Mr. Fine: (Mr. Fine looked up at Krissy and smiled as he handed the book back to her). He said: please visit our website Mr. Fine.com and see my latest book signing events. You will see where I will be attending.

Krissy: (Krissy bent over to grab her book). Thank you so much Mr. Fine I will check your website and visit it this week. Thanks so much for telling me about it.

Mr. Fine: Please feel free to speak to Jane too. Jane enjoys talking to fans. She he doesn't talk down to fans. She's a good listener. Jane will help you and keep you informed. Many blessings to you.

Krissy: Thanks Mr. Fine and likewise. Happy Holidays. Krissy walked away.

Sara was almost ready stepped up to the plate. Sara was nervous and Jean was laughing behind her. Sara stubbed her toe after taking sneaky side photos. She wasn't allowed to be taking any extra photos online. Sara was cracking up as well so was Robert.

Robert: Your sneaky. How's the toe??

Sara: Hah! Hah! Very funny. No, I'm not sneaky. (Sara laughed and whispered) I'm not sneaky, just Slippery! Hee! Hee! (Sara's laughs).

Robert: No. That's the same thing! That's sneaky but hysterical what you did. Don't take anymore sneaky photos of Mr. Fine. Your funny.

Jean: (laughing) need a band aid Sara?

Sara: Stop laughing, I can't take it. You're killing me

Robert: (laughing).

Sara stepped up to Mr. Fine desk trying to refrain from fooling around and laughing. She regained composure.

Sara: Hello, Mr. Fine. My name is Sara Novella.

Mr. Fine: Hello Sara how are you and thank you for coming to my book signing event (exclaimed Mr. Fine). I got a kick out of your comment before and you made me laugh when I was sitting at the platform.

Sara: I'm sorry I disrupted your speech Mr. Fine, but rude fans really upset me and there was no need for that fan to do that to you while you were speaking. I didn't think you heard the comment.

Mr. Fine: It wasn't you who disrupted my speech. I watched you the whole time. It was that fan. He was being a bit abrupt outside as well when I was doing photos. You did nothing wrong Sara.

Sara: Thank you Mr. Fine. It's so nice to meet you. I'm a big fan of the television shows from the eighties and so happy you wrote a book on it. I heard you talking to the fan in front of me about your website and I saw it. It's wonderful. I am so glad you have a fan club that is a part of that website. It's so wonderful to have you here in New York. Thank you for coming out tonight. I loved your book and I hope you will be attending more events. I just got in from upstate New York and here for three days.

Mr. Fine: I will be in LC, NYC tomorrow if you're interested in coming.

Robert: What time in NYC Mr. Fine?

Mr. Fine: At around 5 pm. In the Atrium.

Sara: Do you think we can make it Robert?

Robert: I think so.

Sara: Could you sign my book to Sara, From Mr. Fine.

Mr. Fine: Sure, I can. (Sara did a big smile and started to walk away from Mr. Fine by accident forgetting her book . . . Mr. Fine looked up at Sara.

Mr. Fine: So, do you think you will be able to make it tomorrow evening?

Sara: Turned around after she grabbed the book. Yes. We will probably able to make it. See you tomorrow night.

Chapter 4

A Conversation with Mr. Fine

Wednesday evening at the Center in NYC, fans waited patiently for Mr. Fine as his stretch limousine was parked outside the building. Lisa Smith from Riker's Hospital walked in and people clapped. Lisa Smith is in her 70's. She has silver medium length hair and blue eyes. Lisa looked great. She had on black pants, a white top with a black sequence jacket and heals. She plays one of the longest running characters on Riker's Hospital and plays a wealthy millionaire. Lisa was also a writer on the soap opera Riker's Hospital and journalist. She also worked with Mrs. Fine as well. She travelled with Mrs. Fine and interviewed celebrities. Mrs. Fine worked on the set of Riker's Hospital. She played the part of an upper rich women who lived in San Francisco California, Jean Butler.

Mr. Fine finally took his seat after being outside for several minutes taking photos with his publicist. Mr. Fine also had a detective with him as well standing by a watching everything.

Her name was Laura Dunim. She was about 5 foot 7 a bit chunky with wavy reddish-brown medium length hair with glasses, wearing denim jeans and a black sweatshirt. Laura also works for Mr. Fine at Hotel Chiller. Laura watched the crowd and assisted Mr. Fine where needed. Mr. Fine walked in. He took his seat on the black portable platform next to Lisa Smith. The audience applauded. The chairs were facing Lisa Smith and Richard Fine as the audience continued to applaud.

Mr. Fine: Good evening Lisa, how are you?

Lisa Smith: I am wonderful Mr. Fine How are you?

Mr. Fine: Are there microphones here?

Lisa Smith: Yes, there are. They are bringing them out shortly.

Mr. Fine: (Turns to Lisa) I will chat with the audience for a bit. Several fans came from Washington, DC.

Mr. Fine: said All the way from DC to see me. One fan stated that they were spending the week in New York City.

Washington Fan: Yes. We were at the Revue last night when you were speaking.

Mr. Fine: (The technician finally hands Mr. Fine the microphone.) Thank you, sir. Thank you so much. Then he hands Lisa Smith a microphone as well.

Lisa Smith: Thank You.

The lights in the atrium finally come on as they both have their microphones in their hands. The technician walks away and goes up to the observation booth).

Lisa Smith: (turns towards Mr. Fine) Is your phone working Richard?

Mr. Fine: (Richard turns to Lisa and then taps his microphone). Yes, but I can barely hear the sound. Mr. Fine then looked up at the booth and asked the technician to turn up the sound. Then the sound was better. Mr. Fine turns to the audience and Lisa Smith is laughing.

Mr. Fine: Good evening everyone! The audience clapped for several minutes. After the clapping stopped, he finally introduced Lisa Smith.

Mr. Fine: "This is Lisa Smith." "Lisa was a writer from Riker's Hospital out in California. She flew in today to interview me here in the Atrium.

Mr. Fine: Thank you very much and for making it possible here in the atrium for us to be here. He said if I had to write a book in journalism, it would be on my dear friend "L.S. (turns to Lisa). You would be on the front page."

Lisa Smith: Lisa was humbled as she waived to the audience and the audience clapped. Thank you and thank you for being here with us this evening. It's a pleasure to be anywhere near you.

Mr. Fine: Mr. Fine cracked a big smile. Thank you, Lisa. You are wonderful. Isn't she wonderful?

Mr. Fine turns to the audience and the audience applauds. I am so honored to be here tonight and to be interviewed by you.

Mr. Fine: Turns to the audience: Another evening of speaking in front of wonderful fans. I noticed many of you were at last night's event as well. That's wonderful and thank you for appearing here with us. It's an absolute pleasure to have all of you here.

Lisa Smith: Mr. Fine, what inspired you to write "I Loved Her in The Eighties?"

Mr. Fine: (Mr. Fine for a moment) Then he turned to Lisa.

Mr. Fine: Well Lisa as you know, my wife Leena Fine auditioned for a role on Riker's Hospital back in the Eighties. (Mr. Fine turned to the audience). How many of you watched Riker's Hospital? (the audience starred and clapped). Remember Riker's Hospital is on from 2:30 p.m. to 3pm weekdays?

Well, my wife tried to win tickets as well to the show during events in California. She got my daughter hooked on it as well. One day my wife took my daughter to the set of Riker's Hospital when she was little, and she was almost casted as one of the actor's illegitimate daughters, but I said no. I wanted her to be able to be in school and have a normal life. I never told her she could have had a role on that show.

One time, our name was also put in a charity event, but nothing happened. Mrs. Fine already had the role and was portraying it. When we went, we met Ray Martin before he went nuts. He played a main character on the show. He also announced the raffles for people getting chances to play roles on the set.

Leena already had the role of a wealthy lady or I think it was maid if I'm not mistaken living in San Francisco, California. When Leena started this role, she was asked to write. We were also helping detectives solve a crime as well. I think three murders took place and I was concerned about Leena working on the set.

I was so excited, I kept giving material for Leena to review. I would give pictures to Leena to get autographs. Leena wanted autographs she also wanted to me help write at times and thought I had good sense into what should be done with the show.

One night I set up a fancy dinner outside our patio. I made royal crown of lamb with vegetables of sorts. Then made Potatoes Fine. I called it Potatoes Fine. So, Leena turned around to me and said, "What the hell is Potato's Fine." I was trying to use fancy words to impress Leena, but she got suspicious right away and asked me what I wanted (the audience laughed). So, I finally said it was potatoes in oil. (the audience laughed).

Leena said okay what do you want Richard?? I turned to Mrs. Fine and said I feel that Roy Martin's character should stay, and I should help you write Riker's Hospital from a fans point of view. Mrs. Fine laughed. I will think about it said Mrs. Fine. We were also trying to help detectives solve three murders on Riker's Hospital.

As time passed, Roy Martin was getting angry on the set and thought his character was getting killed off Riker's Hospital. He was flipping out. That was probably why he was killing people so he wouldn't get written off.

Detectives found out Roy Martin killed three people and then tried to kill Leena on the set. While he was attacking Leena, the detective shot him, and he ended up in the hospital. He finally let Leena go. Detectives ended up arresting him and taking him to jail. He was put in the psych ward for several years. (Mr. Fine took a breath for second and reached for his sleeve, fixing his shirt sleeve. He took a deep breath and then stared out into the audience shaking his head.

Mr. Fine: I never understood why he attacked Leena or anyone. What was his motive at that point? Riker's Hospital never wrote him off. Jim Rod took his role after he left and is still playing his character. Jim was a good friend of Roy's. After Roy was caught, the producer came to talk to Roy. Roy recommended Jim Rod for the part for he knew he was going to the psych ward for a while. (Then Mr. Fine looks down and notices that the rug underneath him looks like the one in the Fine house. Then he looks up again).

I used to fool around with Leena in the jacuzzi when she was reading her script. I would practice the lines with her. I would deviate from the script. I would go off and say, "Darling I love you." So, Leena would flip through the pages. You're the only women in my life. So, Leena would flip through the pages and say: "I don't see that here darling." So, I went through the script and said. neither do I . . . so why don't we throw it. We both threw the scripts over our heads (the audience laughed) and started to kiss. (audience laughs again). It was hard being in the hot tub reading lines with a gorgeous woman. I mean who can concentrate? (audience laughs).

I was tired and wanted my wife to cut her hours on Riker's Hospital. She wanted to do the same thing. She did that and just stayed on as a consultant.

There's a brief intermission. Mr. Fine needed to use the bathroom and others needed to stretch their legs for a minute. Lights went down above the platform. They regained their seats. Ten minutes passed and Mr. Fine resumed his seat. The bright yellow lights above the platform came on. The light man filled his pitcher and glass with water. Then he filled Lisa's glass with water as well. Lisa picked up the microphone off the table and so, did Richard Fine. Lisa turned to Richard and spoke into the microphone.

Lisa Smith: We know you like writing on Hollywood Actresses. Is there anything else you are interested in doing besides writing?

Mr. Fine: I would like to visit the pyramids in Egypt which I never did and photograph the country in Africa. I would like to spend some time in Africa and travel all over. I would like write on it and do an educational series on that.

Lisa Smith: If you were asked to write on Riker's Hospital, would you do it?

Mr. Fine: Yes. I would but I would need permission from their head writer. What's his name? (he turns to Lisa). I think its Bill Stigma. Yes. I would write for them.

Lisa Smith: Should we take questions from the audience Richard??

Mr. Fine: Sure, let's get started.

Chapter 5

Questions and Answers with Mr. Fine In N.Y.C.

Mr. Fine: Let's take questions from the audience, shall we??

Lisa Smith: Sure Richard (Lisa was staring at Richard as he looked so very handsome in his black jacket, white shirt and black pants.

So, Richard looks over his shoulder to the gentlemen in the gray shirt and the black tie.

Fan One: Me Sir? (as he is looking down at his tie and pointing to himself).

Mr. Fine: Yes, you sir.

Fan One: Good evening Mr. Fine and thank you much for coming out. I loved your book and I wanted to know if there are any shows in the eighties you wish you would have written on.

Mr. Fine: First of all. Thank you for your kind words and Yes there are still several shows that I would have like to have added to this book, but plan on doing that in the future. The first show is The Big Boat. I am a big fan. I have a ton of photos and took many cruises as well. So that maybe my next story. Maybe I could cruise to Egypt and get a two in one trip book writing deal done. (audience laughs).

Mr. Fine turns towards center stage and smiles. And said hello Sara nice to see you again. (he gives her a big smile)

Sara: *(the detective gives Sara the microphone and Sara takes the microphone from the detective's hands).*

Sara: Hello again Mr. Fine thank you for choosing me. I had a question and I couldn't hear last night at the Revue about Mrs. Fine and Riker's Hospital. I know you would consider writing for Riker's Hospital again. If you did write for Riker's Hospital, would you consider bringing your wife back on the show? Or, bring her on as another character?

Mr. Fine: You're welcome Sara! Sure, I would write her back in the script. Not sure if Mrs. Fine would do the same role after what happen with Roy Martin. But she may consider coming back as a different character. I mean she did enjoy the writing aspect of it and being a free-lance writer for the soap opera. She even wanted to write me in the script, but I knew she would give me a crazy role to play. (the audience laughs) I was glad I was still working part time. I had a real reason to say no thank you. (audience laughs) She would probably make me a busboy or something. (audience laughs again). No, I'm just messing with her.

She has such a god given talent for writing my wife. I don't know where she got it for writing. She could come up with a story in a heartbeat and put it to the camera. I'm not sure I could honestly do that yet. I can do some of it with ideas.

Like I said before when I messed with her one time in the jacuzzi, when she would write a script. I would read it over and fall in love right there. That's why I ended up kissing her in the hot tub all the time. But I knew I had to tone it because then I couldn't practice and kiss her at the same time. I wasted too much time doing that. (audience chuckles). I blame her for making me practice the lines in the jacuzzi.

It was extremely hard to focus sitting with a beautiful lady. (audience laughs). She's incredible. She could do a script in an hour. I was amazed on what she came up with. Amazed! A god given talent for writing my wife has, better than me, but I'm on my way. Thank you so much Sara and I hope to see you at future book signings. (he points to another fan). He gives Sara a handsome smirk.

Sara: Blushed and giggled to Robert

Fan # 3: (the pretty detective took the microphone out of Sara's hands and gave it to another fan). Good evening Mr. Fine I was wondering if you are planning on anymore book signing events. If so? When and where??

Mr. Fine: Yes. I will be doing more book signings in the next two months. I will be travelling up and down the East Coast from now until December. As a matter of speaking I brought a list of dates with me and made copies. I figured someone would be asking. I will have my webmaster posts them. It should also be up on my website at the end of the week.

Mr. Fine: I know some of you won't be getting your book signed. I remember seeing you last night at the review. How many of you were at the review and did will not be getting their book signed?

(Several audiences members raised their hands). Mr. Fine handed his copies to the pretty detective and she gives everyone in the audience a copy of dates where Mr. Fine will be appearing. The detective handed fan four a copy.

Fan #4: Pretty Bitch.

Detective: (Pulled back and walked away ignoring him, handing out the rest of the copies to fans).

Mr. Fine: Turns to the detective and got suspicious. Are you okay? Did he say something?

Mr. Fine turned and looked at Fan four and thought he looked familiar.

Detective: I'm fine said the detective. It's okay.

Sara: Robert look it's that guy from last night.

Robert: You're paranoid. No wait. You're right. Don't say anything. Yeah, it's him remember the eye looked funny.

Sara: (Sara couldn't contain herself). That is ASSWIPE! (one guy chuckled behind Sara) Some are going up to get copies of Mr. Fine book signing dates. I'm going to snap some shots.

So, Sara started filming around with her camera.

Mr. Fine: Turned and smirked at Sara and knew Sara saw the same person as he watched her film him. Mr. Fine was become impressed with Sara by the minute. Robert was quietly filming him as he was saying stuff. (Mr. Fine Turns to audience) That concludes our panel discussion for tonight.

Robert: I told you to keep quiet that guy is a creep. I think he said something to the detective.

Sara: I heard something like bitch but not sure. His eyes are weird looking. Does he know her??

Robert: He said something it could have been bitch. Sounded like it but cannot be sure. I want to come to the next couple of book signings to see if he is following him. Not sure if I can make them all.

Richard was gathering the other copies and putting it back in his briefcase. Lisa Smith was starting to clean up her things as well.

Lisa Smith: That concludes our panel discussion tonight Mr. Fine. Thank You so much for coming.

Mr. Fine: Thank you so much for the interview Lisa. It's been a great evening.

The audience applauds

Mr. Fine: Turned to the audience with great expression and gratitude thanking each one for coming out to see him tonight and said if you want your book signed, I would be over by the entrance way in the room over there. (he pointed).

Mr. Fine: Finally, he stood up on the dais and so did Lisa Smith. The fans in the audience got up as well and continued to clap.

Many headed towards the separate room for the autograph signing.

Sara and Robert were ready to leave. Robert was in a rush to get back home. They had to catch a train. They traveled by train and it was getting late. Mr. Fine was helping Lisa Smith off the stage. Reporters and fans were taking pictures of Mr. Fine. Most of the fans went to get their booked signed. Mr. Fine was shaking hands with other fans and reporters. He waved to Sara and Robert as they were leaving the atrium.

Chapter 6

The Emerging Stalker

There was a second short intermission before Mr. Fine was signing autographs. During intermission Laura went on break to the restroom.

Laura walked down a long corridor. It was a bit dim the lights and no one was around. She had to use the ladies' room. She went to the ladies' room in the stall. She didn't know she was being followed. Laura went into the bathroom and into the stall to use the toilet. She heard the door open then heard loud clanking footsteps. It sounding like men's dress shoes and the heal hitting the tile of the floor. The lights went out.

There are six stalls and Laura's were the furthest away from the door. Laura peeks through the hole of the stall to see if she can see what he looks like. All she sees is a guy with a weird looking eye and the buckles on his boots. Laura thought she saw him with a phone in his hand dialing but couldn't be sure.

Laura: (She locks the door and grabs her phone to dial 911) I'm calling the police she exclaimed!

Stalker: He puts on his black gloves one by one and pulls each one up against his wrist. Bitch! He exclaimed. Whispering loudly. Bitch! with labored breathing. Then the stalker picks up the phone himself to mock Laura and dials. Then he says "bitch" on the phone. He hangs it up and heads towards Laura.

Laura: Police are on their way she exclaimed! Laura was extremely frightened. She pulls out her gun for back up. Laura made sure the receiver of her gun was fully loaded as it clicked in position to shoot. Laura aimed it at the front door of the stall. I also have a gun.

Laura looked down and saw his dark boot shoes with buckles. Laura peeks again through the stalls and sees the stalker putting a black device looking like a phone in his pocket.

Stalker: Then pulls out his handkerchief and rolls it and stretches it out spinning it straight out until it's rolled up horizontally as if he is going to strangle her. Then he tugs sideways and laughs heading for the stall where Laura is.

Laura: Come in and I will shoot.

Stalker: (the bathroom door slams open and he runs out).

Laura called for security at the center and a guard came asking questions. Mr. Fine was getting curious as to where Laura was for it was a half hour already and she had not returned to the signing tables. Laura gave the security guard the information and then she said she went to assist Mr. Fine. Mr. Fine was at the front of the atrium signing books. Security took information and it took about forty minutes before Laura returned. Laura finally returned and the line was just finishing up.

Mr. Fine: Are you okay?

Laura: I am fine. Someone came into the bathroom just now and scared me. One security guard took my report and information.

Mr. Fine: Was it the same person who was in the audience.

Laura: I couldn't see him.

Mr. Fine: I have a few more autographs to sign. After I finish up, I will have my chauffeur drop you off. Why don't I take you home tonight and drop you off?

Laura: Thank you Mr. Fine.

Chapter 7

Meanwhile Back at The House

Richard finally came home from his book signing event. When he walked in Whisky was sitting and wagging his tail with Richard's necktie in his mouth.

Scotch got sneaky fast and made a quick disappearing act. Scotch headed for the hills and made a beeline for the other room. He disappeared into another room fast when he saw Mr. Fine come home. The dog couldn't be bothered, and left Whisky to get in trouble. Richard wondered if Scotch was hiding because of the missing necktie.

Scotch dropped the tie and first gave two barks, then three barks.

Leena came in from the kitchen and smiled. She knew she took photos of the dog and put a tie around Whisky's neck so Scotch wouldn't get in trouble. She showed Mr. Fine.

Richard dropped his luggage. Leena showed Richard the pictures of the dogs and he laughed and looked at Whisky. Whisky hid his nose in the tie and knew he was in trouble with Mr. Fine.

He grabbed both of Leena's arms and pulled her up to his chest tightly and kissed her for about ten minutes. The dog dipped his nose into the couch and growled in jealousy. There lips were so tight it was hard for anyone to distract them.

Mrs. Fine got her index finger and wiped the lipstick off Richard's lips.

Mrs. Fine looked so pretty it was hard for Mr. Fine to take his eyes off his wife. She looked so good. So very slender with and sexy with her hourglass waistline. Mrs. Fine was wearing a white skirt, red shirt, white jacket and black shoes. She just came back from Bobs and had gotten her hair colored and cut. She also shopped at Taylors in Beverly Hills and bought a sexy lingerie for the evening to wear for her husband. She smelled so good.

Richard: Did you get your hair colored at Bobs?

Leena: Yes, I did Darling. Especially for you. (taps Richard on the side). Say why don't we have dinner together and leave the bags there. I will wash your clothes later.

Richard: Thank you darling? Did you book our private dinner for the Convention Center next week in Baltimore, Maryland?

Leena: Yes, I did. Your publicist Meg Rivera got back to me and gave me all the names who were going to dinner. I put in the reservation for Thursday at 6:30 pm. We get done signing autographs early at 4 p.m. I thought it was best to do dinner Thursday.

Richard: You're so smart. He kisses her once on the lips.

Leena: I know . . . As she continues to wipe her lipstick off his lips.

Richard: Gives two kisses. What would I do without you?

Leena: You would have Whisky and Scotch eating your ties. Whisky's head is up staring at them kissing wagging his tail for attention, but Mr. Fine is ignoring Whisky and kissing Mrs. Fine.

Richard: Kisses her a fourth time on the lips. Very funny. Whisky is definitely guilty. He then puts his arms around her. Want to go upstairs for a little while? (Whisky growls again). What about dinner?

Leena: It can wait. He kisses her for another ten minutes.

Richard: He puts his fingers through her hair and plays with her hair. Let me put it on warm or turn it off. We can come back later.

Leena: Hurry up. Richard brought his luggage upstairs to the bedroom and started unpacking, putting his clothes in the hamper. Whisky followed him wagging his tail.

Leena: (shakes her head at the dog). He Eats my husband's tie and then follows him to the kitchen. That dog is always hungry. What to do with that dog! Mrs. Fine exclaims! The dog doesn't wait for me.

Richard, Leena and Whisky head upstairs.

Leena and Richard decided to stay in bed a bit longer fooling around kissing and so forth. The dog was on the floor on Richard's side by the bedroom. A few hours passed by. They both stop. Leena shut the lights. Both turnover and fell to sleep.

Chapter 8

Night Stalker

Leena and Richard fell asleep for a few hours after their romantic time in bed. Leena got up. She grabbed her long white satin robe from her walk-in closet and put it on. Then she stood by the window. She stood by the window and stared out by her Mercedes Benz.

Richard rolled over towards Leena side and went to put his arms around his wife, felt nothing. He rolled opposite direction and turned on the lamp. He saw her standing by the window. He turned off the lamp and got out of bed to go stand by her in the dark. He stood behind her with his arms around her and asked if she was okay. He massaged her shoulders so gently on top. Mrs. Fine leaned back against him.

Leena: Yes. I have something to tell you.

Leena: Richard.

Richard: What is it darling?

Leena: Well, last night something weird happened but I didn't want to alarm you.

Richard: What happened?

Leena: I was alone sitting on the couch with Whisky when the phone rang. I picked up the phone and the person whispered bitch and said next time it's you. This was around 9 p.m. last night. I thought maybe the person had the wrong phone number.

Richard: (Thought about the detective being attacked and maybe he thought it was meant for his wife Leena and wanted Leena instead. Richard said nothing) Do you have a number?

Leena: Why darling?

Richard: Well my detective was attacked last night in NYC. I took her home. I'm wondering if the attacker didn't call you afterwards.

Leena: I didn't take a number. I deleted it because he said it was the wrong number.

Richard: I will see if I can call the phone company tomorrow to get the number.

Richard: Okay darling. Then I can give it to the police officer to see where he is from.

Leena: (Looks out the window) Darling, did you see that?

Richard: See what? (as he gets closer to her) I'm too busy staring at a gorgeous lady.

Leena: Richard! I think someone is outside. He looked like he was by the bush.

Richard: I'll go check. You stay here and lock the doors. Where's the dog he asked. (Then Richard heard Whisky barking at the front door).

(Richard hysterically put on his wife's mink over his red silk pajamas and turned on the lights in the hallway and went downstairs to see what Whisky was up to).

Richard: Come on my little doggie, come on boy. (He grabbed the dog) by the color and walked through the kitchen to the back where the car was parked). Whisky didn't really want to go at first. He looked a bit uptight at first. But then he moved as Richard put his leash on and tugged at his collar.

Richard took him outside and he walked all around the premise a bit to see if anyone was outside. Richard didn't see anyone, so he brought Whisky back inside. Leena sat up in bed waiting for Richard. The doors were locked. Leena heard knocking at the bedroom door.

Richard: (started knocking at the door) Darling open it's me.

Leena: (Went to the door and opened it up). Richard came in.

Richard: No one was out there. I took Whisky. We walked around to the front and back twice but saw no one. Maybe it was an animal.

Leena: Standing on Two Legs?? You're probably right darling. Let's go to bed tomorrow I will wash your clothes and re- pack them for the weekend for our trip to Baltimore.

Richard: Okay darling.

Both of them go back to bed.

Leena*:* Turns to her side of the light and leans over towards Richard. Richard shuts his side of the light and doses off to sleep. Leena gets up and leans over Richard.

Leena: Darling. As she plays with his hair. She put her index finger above his ear playing with his hair.

Richard: He opens one eyelid. In a deep tone calm voice. What is it darling?

Leena: Where are the dogs?

Richard: At the edge of the bed. Whisky barked twice!

Mrs. Fine leaned over and kissed Mr. Fine. Mr. Fine was tired, but he responded rather suddenly and romantically. Their kissing went on for about several minutes and then they both fell asleep.

Chapter 9

The Convention Center

A week almost past and Thursday arrived.

The Fines were on the plane to Baltimore Maryland to the Convention Center at the Harbor Inn. On their private jet Mr. Fine was hoping Whisky and Scotch didn't take any more of his things from his suitcase. Mrs. Fine double checked everything and made sure the dogs were downstairs this time, especially Whisky. Mrs. Fine knew that Whisky had a stash of their things outside and likes to hide ties. One time, Mrs. Fine found chewed shoes, socks, tissue paper and pillowcases underneath the flowerpot on the back porch. Also, in a carriage outside.

Another time, Mrs. Fine bought Mr. Fine a pair of black cowboy boots for their ranch vacation with buckles. Whisky as smart as he was found the side where the buckles were. He chewed off the buckles on Mr. Fine's shoes and hid it. Mrs. Fine couldn't believe a small dog could chew on so many things.

She never told Mr. Fine because she knew Whisky would be in trouble. Mrs. Fine found out about it before Mrs. Fine came home from work and glued the buckles back on. Mrs. Fine knew everything was okay this time, as she sat back on the plane looking over her checklist, finalizing plans.

Mr. Fine knew many fans were coming to this book signing event. He was told by Meg his publicist that many fans from his Facebook group told her they were coming. Many from the center in New York. He couldn't wait as he was coming in for a landing and speaking with his publicist at the same time.

The wheels underneath the plane came out and finally hit the pavement. Mrs. Fine's jet landed outside the private section of the airport. They grabbed their luggage from their cabin . . .

Their flight attendant opened the door and the long stairs landed to the ground where they existed downstairs into the airport terminal. Mr. and Mrs. Fine took the long escalator upstairs and towards the exit doors where their chauffeur was waiting to take them to the convention center Harbor Inn Hotel Convention Center.

The chauffeur travelled through to Baltimore Parkway. While driving, the beautiful scenic route was very relaxing. Every turn there were beautiful green trees and countryside. Everywhere you looked there was something to see.

Historic towns and rural landscapes gave sense that this was going to be a wonderful experience. As they passed through the historic town of Baltimore, Maryland, Mrs. Fine thought about how well manicured the historic gothic homes were, with its pristine designs and outdoor sculptures.

Mrs. Fine was wondering how far back these homes dated. It was also the town of her favorite mysterious poet and she knew his burial place wasn't too far away. Mrs. Fine also wanted the chauffeur to turn off to one of streets where there was taverns, boutiques and cafes so she could go shopping. Mr. Fine had a deadline and thought about staying a couple of days at the hotel so his wife could visit them later.

After passing through the valley green hills and river valley, the Fines finally arrived at the Convention Center Hotel in Baltimore, Maryland. Their chauffeur pulled right up to the redbrick road circular entrance and door. He got out and opened the door. The Fines stepped out of the limousine, tipped the chauffeur.

The concierge service attendant took their luggage, ticketed it, and checked it in. Then he put it on a rolling cart and brought through the front entrance of the desk. Mr. Fine took off his jacket and put it over his shoulder. Then, he put his arms around his wife and kissed her before entering the hotel. They walked into the hotel and checked in at the front desk.

Receptionist: Good afternoon can I help you?

Mr. Fine: Yes, my name is Richard Fine. I have a reservation for Thursday thru Tuesday night here at the Convention Center.

Receptionist: Aren't you The Mr. Fine who wrote "I Loved Her in The Eighties?"

Mr. Fine: Yes. That would be me.

Receptionist: I just want you to know I love your book and your wife is gorgeous.

Mrs. Fine: Thank you.

Receptionist: I will pull your name up on my computer to see if your room is ready. As she is going through the names, the concierge attendant straightens out Mr. Fine's bags. Oh! Here we are. Yes, your room is ready.

(She reaches for the draw to open it and pull out the two room keys and puts them on top of the counter).

Receptionist: You are room 170 which is around the corner and down the hall. Hold on I just want to tell you what you owe. . . . that will be $1000 altogether.

This is a gift bag for all celebrities this weekend attending our convention and autograph show.

Mr. Fine: (Puts his arms around his wife and starts kissing his wife while they are printing out copies).

Receptionist: (Trying to clear her throat to get Mr. Fine's attention and smirked).

Mr. Fine: (Turns to the receptionist). I'm sorry, I have a difficult time concentrating when I'm surrounded by gorgeous women.

Mrs. Fine: Darling? (She rubs and squeezes his elbow with her hand).

Receptionist: (blushes). Would I be able to come downstairs later and get your autograph Mr. Fine and Mrs. Fine? I remember seeing you on Riker's Hospital.

Mr. Fine: I will give you my autograph right now.

Mrs. Fine: So, will I.

Receptionist: Hold on I have a pen. (The receptionist hands Mr. and Mrs. Fine a pen with notepad).

Mr. Fine: Who do I make it to?

Receptionist: Tammy.

Mr. Fine: There you go Tammy. Don't wait online if you don't have to.

Tammy: Thank you Mr. Fine.

Mrs. Fine: Here you go Tammy.

Tammy: Thank you Mrs. Fine. Here's your receipt. Hold on one second. *Tammy went into the computer and put in an 20% discount towards Mr. and Mrs. Fine's bill.*

I took off 20% off the room and added it to your bill. I deducted it from your card and added back the discount.

Mr. Fine: How Sweet. Thank you, Tammy.

Mrs. Fine: Thank you, Tammy, that was really nice!

Mr. and Mrs. Fine went to their stateroom and unpacked their stuff.

Chapter 10

Meanwhile Travelling to Fines

Meanwhile back on the train while passing through the state of Washington, DC., Sara and Robert were headed to the Convention Center to see Mr. and Mrs. Fine. Sara was so excited for she knew in a few hours she would be having dinner with the Fines. Robert wasn't having dinner but decided to rest upstairs. He had work to do for business.

Robert and Sara were sitting in the four-bucket seat on the train. Robert was going through his camera and getting his camera ready. Robert and Sara had been on the train for about four hours now and had two hours to go. The train took them through the scenic valleys and bridges of Maryland. Robert was facing Sara and then he cracked up after looking at his camera. He started cracking jokes. He also uploaded a bunch of photos of Mr. Fine's book signings on a flash drive twice and gave one flash drive to Sara.

Robert: (shows Sara the camera) You lied to Mr. Fine. (laughs). I uploaded a bunch of pictures and a set of pictures for you. You never know what's in these photos.

Sara: You're such a troublemaker. I did not lie! Your sister lied.

Robert: You both lied and you both were sneaky. You took sneaky photos of Mr. Fine when you shouldn't have. The speaker in charge at the Revue said no extra pictures were allowed, especially while signing autographs. What do Sara and Jean do? They both take pictures when they are not supposed to.

Sara: (laughs) I had nothing to do with it. (laughs) I mean I knew he was sitting alone and told your sister, but I didn't take the photo. I just said he was there and we can get a shot. That was it.

Robert: (laughs) You're killing me. (figure of speech). You did have something to do with it! You pointed him out and Jean took a photo. (laughs).

Sara: I had something to do with it but I didn't. I can't explain it.

Robert: Laughs.

Passenger 1: (is sitting opposite side of Robert and laughing). Guilty!

Robert: Guilty! (as he smirks and laughs) Hee hee!

Sara: (Laughs) Now wait a minute. That's Two against one. I didn't lie to Mr. Fine. I just fibbed.

Robert: No! (laughs) you lied.

Sara: No, it wasn't the whole truth but I didn't lie.

Passenger 1: Laughing.

Sara: (Turns to the passenger and says) If you tell a little lie isn't that called a fib?

Passenger 1: No, a fib is a white lie. A little one but if you continue to fib then you're lying.

Robert: That's right. Many fibs are lie.

Robert, Sara, and Passengers were discussing and joking the difference between a fib and a lie.

Sara: It's not lying it's not the whole truth. But if you don't tell the whole truth it's not lying.

Passenger 1: (turns to Robert) If you don't tell the truth it's a lie.

Robert: That's right. If you're not telling the truth and your being sneaky it's a lie.

Sara: That's two against one not good! (Sara laughs).

Passenger and Robert: Both laugh. Let's ask the other passengers.

Sara: Laughs.

Two hours finally passed and their trained stopped downtown in Baltimore. Robert and Sara grabbed their luggage from the top compartments and waits patiently for the train to stop.

When the train came to a full stop the doors opened. Passengers were lined up going out the door. Passengers wouldn't allow Sara or Robert to cut in. Everyone was in a rush to get into the train station terminal and grab their taxi or car, or just catch another train. So, Sara and Robert waited patiently and finally Sara tried to cut in front of one of the passengers.

Sara: (Steps in front of the passenger).

Passenger #2: (Whispers in heavy breathing) bi hi hi hitch . . . Passenger walks pass her and exits out the door.

Sara: Robert wait.

Robert: What is it?

Sara: Did you see that guy?

Robert: Yes, but he left.

Sara: Did you hear what he said?

Robert: No, no I did not. Did he say something to you??

Sara: Yet he called me a bitch and whispered if. Like he said to the detective in NYC.

Robert: You're paranoid. That guy is weird.

Sara: Well so is the other guy at L. C. It really looked like him. Do you think he could be going to see Mr. Fine at the Convention Center Hotel? He had that weird looking eye.

Robert: I don't know it could be a possibility. That's why I came this weekend. I did say he could be following him. We will find out. Come on Sara let's go. If he is going to try something, we can tell Mr. Fine. We will see him soon.

Robert and Sara grabbed their luggage and walked off the train. They exited off the train and pass the monitors up the long flight of cemented stairs into the bus terminal. Then they passed train terminal in downtown Baltimore.

When they stepped outside the station their cab was waiting to take them to the hotel in Baltimore. Robert and Sara hopped into the limousine and headed for the Convention Center. Over the hilly roads and bridges, they went. The trees were so beautiful as their colors of brown, yellow and gold glistened for miles on end. The fall leaves really have peaked this season and clinging to the trees instead of the ground. Nothing seemed more relaxing than a scenic ride to the Maryland scenic byways during a long stretch. Some of the oldest towns were so quaint.

Sara and Robert thought it was such a peaceful drive through the valley and marshes. As Sara looked left of her, she can the mountains which stood like 3000 feet high or it seemed. Then Sara wanted to ask the drive what consists of a fib.

Sara: (I have a question?)

Driver: Sure? What is it? The driver thought maybe Sara was going to ask about sightseeing spots.

Sara: Is a lie a fib.

Robert: (Laughed). Here we go again! (turns to driver) I'd recommend ear plugs!

Driver: (Laughed) I think I'm glutton for punishment. A fib is a lie. (he turns to Rob).

Robert: I told her that. If you tell a lot of fibs it's a lie.

Driver and Robert continue the conversation about fibbing for the next ten minutes.

Driver: My mother always called a fib a little white lie.

Robert: I say if you lied you lied whether it's big or small a lie is a lie. Robert laughs.

Driver: You have a dictionary on you. Up we are here.

Robert: Saved by the hotel.

Driver: Laughs.

The driver pulls into the Convention Center Hotel. The chauffeur gets Sara and Robert their bags.

Robert tips the driver.

Sara: You know I'm meeting a fan here in about five minutes.

Robert: Yes, I know. It's about three o clock our rooms should be ready.

Sara and Robert grabbed their luggage and they went into the sliding doors of the *hotel to the front desk and checked in. Robert decided to go to his room. He was next door to Sara's room.*

Sara waited for the fan from the Facebook page group. All their luggage was delivered to their room.

Sara sat in the entry way of the hotel. It looked so pretty with its pink quartz crystal like balls hanging from the ceiling and open glass roof top. She sat for a few seconds. Then she saw her fan friend Mindy.

She gave her a big hug and hello. They both checked in at the door and went to their room to freshen up. The autograph show was downstairs. Mr. and Mrs. Fine were signing autographs for another hour in a half before they were through.

Chapter 11

Counterplotting Mr. Fine's Death

Sara and Mindy were in Room 222.

The guy who was stalking Mr. Fine in NYC, was in room 230, which was down the hall. His name was Roy. He was next door to Sara and Mindy. Sara didn't know it, neither did Robert. Robert's room was across the way.

Roy was a bit obsessed with Richard Fine and started developing an obsession for Leena Fine. He felt that Leena shouldn't be left alone and that he would console her after Richard Fine was dead.

As he was unpacking, he turned on his television and saw the broadcast of Richard and Leena Fine They were doing a news interview which took place downstairs at the convention room. The film all must have been about two hours old.

Roy looks up at the 42-inch screen TV to see if he sees himself. Then he realizes it was filmed earlier than he had thought.

Reporter: Some of our biggest stars in television are in Baltimore County. The Convention Center is running on high this weekend with an autograph signing show at the Convention Center in Maryland.

Writers, celebrities and television royalty showed up as the red carpet rolled out for two new celebrities Richard and Leena Fine. Celebrities like Jim Rod, Marie St. John, and many other glamourous ladies are here for the weekend.

As the news reporter turns, he walks up to Richard and Leena Fine.

Reporter: Welcome! Welcome to Baltimore and to the Convention Center for the first time. How are you doing?

Mrs. Fine looked so pretty and slender in her blue slacks, pants and scarf. Her medium brown wavy hair touching her shoulders.

Mr. Fine didn't' look to shabby himself with his blue shirt and Jacket, both so warming and humbled to be there. Mr. Fine's blue eyes and silver hair with brown streaks matched his shirt.

Mr. Fine: Thank you! (As he bows forward towards the reporter) I'm terrific. This is Mrs. Fine.

Reporter: How do you do?

Mrs. Fine: So far. So good.

Reporter: So good to have you here in Maryland and promoting your latest book.

Mr. Fine: Thank you again Sir. Yes, I will be autographing my latest book "I Loved Her in The Eighties." Many celebrities are also here from that book that I have written about. I'm very excited about that. Mrs. Fine and myself will be meeting and greeting fans, for the first time. Some have come for the second and third time too. This is an exciting time for all of us.

The fans have been great and patient. Let's face it, I'm new at this celebrity stuff. But I thought I'd give it a shot. My wife did it in the eighties. I thought I'd do it now. *(He kisses Mrs. Fine).*

Richard: (mamma!) He goes. (looks back at the reporter) I get very distracted with gorgeous women like my wife. (he rubs her arm).

Reporter: (laughs). Thank you, Mr. and Mrs. Fine. Thank you for coming to the Convention Center.

Mr. Fine: You're welcome. Mr. and Mrs. Fine head towards their booth and the film is cut.

Roy was in his room and is watching the news cast on television. He was watching Mr. and Mrs. Fine being interviewed for the first time. He got angrier by the minute while sitting in bed and watching the Fines on television being interviewed. He was fuming in high jealousy and rage.

Roy: (begins to flip out. He starts to kiss the photo of Leena).

Mamma!!! Mm mwah!!! Mm mwah! Wah! Wah! Wah! Richard how about that! (Then he takes an army serrated pocket knife which had all kinds of blades attached to it, and starts slicing up Richard's picture). He picks up Leena's picture. You should be married to me. ME! ME! ME! As his rage gets louder and louder, he shakes her photo . . . then carves out bitch on Richard's picture with one of the tools of his pocket knife. Phone rings . . . he calms down.).

Roy: Hello (behavior goes back to normal).

Cindy: Have you decided to hurt Mr. Fine this weekend??

Roy: Nc. Just tormenting him until he has nightmares? (I think! Scratching his head and laughing). There I feel better now. But he's pissing me off getting on television and shit. What the heck is wrong with him. Why does he get to go on television and brag???? He will probably be at the bar in about an hour.

Cindy: There's another book signing event?

Roy: Where?

Cindy: Graveyard Theater in Parsippany New Jersey. Many actors from the television shows from the eighties will be there. Mr. and Mrs. Fine will be there too.

Roy: Really? Give me the hotel information.

Cindy: No worries. I booked us just in case.

Roy: Yeah, beautiful. I heard something like that in NYC but I was getting yelled at by security. I almost got kicked out and couldn't get the dates. (ha!! Ha! Mr. Fine..Got Them Now..) Okay I will talk to later. He hangs up the phone and starts talking to himself. I need to make a list on what I want to do to Mr. Fine. Yes. I have my white board here. *(talking out loud to himself).*

First, he is really pissing me off and at the wrong time. Is there a pad here?? I know I bought stuff and white board with dry erase marker as well. He took out some pens and stuff. Still talking to himself. I have to get busy. I have to jot some stuff down. I haven't got much time I have to be downstairs in an hour.

Roy knows he has work to be done. He's headed downstairs in an hour to see if he can cause some trouble for the Fines.

Roy took out his whiteboard and dry erase markers. He sat on the bed. He had different colors to and rainbow pack set he bought on sale. He made a list and brainstormed some ideas on what he wanted to do to Richard Fine. Roy writes down "Ideas on How to Hurt Richard Fine." Underneath on the white board he starts to make his list starts humming and singing . . .do do do dit dit do..kill Richard Fine.

Let's See Writes:

#1 Trip him in the elevator. (boring)

#2 Knock on his doors at night and send him a bottle of rat poison.

#3 Send him a box of candy with raid sprayed on it. "how would Mr. Fine React but!" (Roy put an asterisk by here because he wasn't sure.

#4 Pull the fire alarm and shoot him.

#5 Call 911 then shoot him, or

#6 just continue to torment him.

#7 Write threatening Notes!

#8 Prank call his room!

#9 Send notes

#10 Harass him online signing autographs. So many options to choose from, Roy didn't know what to do. I like #10 as he looks at the board and puts 2 red asterisks by Roy saved his white board and put it away in his suitcase. The black asterisk was a reminder for no and red meant yes. He hid all the photos so no one would see what he was doing. He grabs Mr. Fine's photo from the book signing event.

Roy: So many ideas to choose from. Which one am I going to do? Don't worry Richard, I will figure out something and puts the knife through his photo.

Roy: (talking to himself out loud). But at least I'm am calmer than I was before and saner. I don't know what to do.

I like #10 as he looks at the board and puts two red asterisks by the number

Roy saved his white board and put it away in his suitcase. The black asterisk was a reminder for no and red meant yes. He hid all the photos so no one would see what he was doing. He grabs Mr. Fine's photo from the book signing event.

Roy: So many ideas to choose from. Which one am I going to do? Don't worry Richard, I will figure out something and puts the knife through his photo.

Then he takes a picture of Mrs. Fine and draws red lipstick on it and kisses the photo.

So beautiful to kiss to look at he said, but you should be with me and I have to fix it so you will. I think I'm going to hang you up on the wall.

He kissed the photo several times. He just kept his lips against her for several minutes. Then he hung the photo on the wall. He took a piece of scotch tape and taped it to the mirror above the dresser in front of him.

Chapter 12

Dinner with The Fines

It was around 4:30 pm. Richard and Leena finished packing up their table. Richard looked up and thought she saw Roy.

Leena: What is it darling??

Richard : That guy over there. He was at the Revue and gave me a hard time. I think it's him but I cannot be sure.

Leena: I heard him say he was going to the bar. He was over here before and I thought he was strange. He just stared at me. His eyes are weird looking.

Richard: Yeah, I think that's him. Let's go to the bar before dinner we have some time. You go first and I will disguise myself.

Leena: Okay. I am headed to the bar or should I dress in something sexy??

Richard: Put that sexy black dress or black pants suit outfit on. If you bought your tight sexy satin pants, wear those.

Leena: Okay darling will do. I will go to the room and get dressed really fast.

Richard: I'm going to buy a costume next door and come to the bar. See you in about fifteen minutes.

Leena: Okay darling.

Leena walked back to her hotel room. She put on her black shirt and tight satin pants outfit, red belt with chains and red heels. She brushed her hair. She was happy that she got her hair re-done and twice in one week. She wanted it a little shorter and bouncy for the trip to Baltimore. She puts on her makeup and brushed her hair. Then she put on lipstick and perfume. She grabbed her black handbag and she grabbed her room key. Then, walked down to the bar. Mrs. Fine sat at the stool and put her hand bag on top. She grabbed money out of her black purse with the red crystal hearts on them.

The Bar Jukebox was playing seventies disco music on it.

Leena: Bartender, I will have a tequila please?

Bartender: Coming up.

Leena: Okay, great thank you.

Bartender: Here by yourself. Your too pretty to be sitting at a bar alone.

Leena: I'm so flattered. Well aren't you the ladies' man of the night!

Richard: (walks in with tight denim jeans. He also wore a belt with chains around his jeans, blue shirt and black jacket. sunglasses and a beard. He had one earring from his ear). He puts his hand around her waist and feels her up and down). Hey! Hey! good looking what got cooking?) I thought I was your ladies' man! I guess I will have the same bartender.

Leena: Careful all our chains may lock, then what will happen. (Bartender dropped his glass and went to pick it up.)

Roy: (Comes in with a cowboy hat and puts his arms around Leena). How ya been darling? You can have me for a ladies' man.

Leena: (Leena turns) I'm sorry have we met?

Roy: You don't remember Me he exclaimed?

Richard: Hey cowboy, I don't think she remembers you, so why don't you waddle on back to the barn where you came from.

Roy: Why don't you waddle on back yourself. You look familiar and he pulls at Richard's beard. Then he picks at both of Richard's cheeks. He pinches one check. So cute...

Richard: Took the cowboy by the arm and twisted his arm in back. Then he leaned him over the counter bar. (what did you say)?

Roy: Alright! All right I will let her go. I promise. (His hat falls over the bar to where the bottles are and the bartender bends over to pick it up).

Richard: Then get your you know what on out of here.

Bartender: Hey you here's your hat. (Roy took off his hat and put it on his head).

Looks to Mr. and Mrs. Fine That will be twenty dollars.

Richard: (feels ups Leena's waist). What about going to my place and listening to some sounds hot mama!

Leena: Maybe. (as she turns towards Richard). But we have a dinner party, remember??

Richard: That's right I almost forgot. You are meeting them first right.

Leena: Yes darling. I will go now to greet them.

Richard: (pays the bartender). How about that. Always something. Can't ever get my beautiful wife alone.

Bartender: That's the way it goes.

Leena sat at the bar a bit longer and saw the fans lining up for dinner around the corner.

Mrs. Fine walks in and the girls are all sitting around the table. Sara is sitting at the table with five other girls. About twenty girls showed up for Mr. Fine's dinner and for Mr. Fine to greet his fans. There were five girls at each table. Mrs. Fine came in to chat with the girls and let them know Richard will be running late. Richard was next door to having some drinks and talking to some of the actors from Riker's Hospital. Jim Rod and Rachael Goldstein had walked in. He wanted to catch up with them awhile.

Mrs. Fine walked in and looked all around both ways. She waved to everyone as she smiled and walked over to the table by the mirror. Mrs. Fine finally figured out that Mr. Fine is probably going to pull a stunt with the fans and have fun with his new fans in about a half hour.

Mrs. Fine went around each table and met every one of their hands. She shucks hands with everyone. So glamorous and pretty as her hair bounced from one side to the next while she was walking around the tables.

She sat at one table and talked about her special fundraising projects that she came up with. She thanked the fans for coming and told them that part of the money for their dinner is going towards her favorite wildlife organization. She thanked the fans for their support. Then she shared some stories with her fans.

Mrs. Fine sat at another table and chatted about herself being on Riker's Hospital.

Many fans came to the table to listen to Mrs. Fine speak on Riker's Hospital. Mrs. Fine chatted about the time she got attacked in the studio and how she sprained her back after the attack.

She stated after Roy Martin was arrested, she was taken to the hospital because she had bruised and cut her low back. She hurt it by the door on the set. When Mr. Fine was trying to get the knife out of his hand, he hurt her by holding her in a strange position. She said she went to physical therapy for several weeks and continued to write for the show. Many wanted to know if she was coming back to play the part of the same character.

Sara asked her about that and she said she wasn't sure if she would do that again. But she would go back to do a different role. Sara told Mrs. Fine that's what your husband said as well. Then another fan asked what time Mr. Fine was coming to dinner. Mrs. Fine said he should be coming anytime. I'm not sure what's taking him so long.

Mrs. Fine asked to be excused. She wanted to see what was taking Richard so long. She got up and walked towards the door. She saw him chatting with Jim Rod and Rachael Goldstein from Riker's Hospital. Mrs. Fine looked over at the bar and saw Rachael Goldstein with some guy. Jim Rod was standing there. Rachael looked up and waved to Mrs. Fine.

Mrs. Fine went in and talked to Rachael for a second. She said that Richard went back to the hotel room to change his clothes and use the bathroom. He did get an emergency call on something. Mrs. Fine thought maybe there was news on her daughter Lynn. So, she thanked Rachael and went back inside to tell fans to eat dinner and that Mr. Fine will be in shortly. He got a last-minute call.

Fans shortly got up and went to the buffet in the separate room There was an array of delicious food ranging from chicken, roast beef, pasta, meatloaf, mash potatoes, vegetables, assorted rolls, lasagna, tomato sauce, gravy. There was a salad bar with three or four different salads to choose from and dressings. There was also a dessert bar with chocolate cake, cheese cake, rice pudding.

There was also fruit salad, cookies, pies, and pudding with an ice cream Sunday bar. Fans were eating dinner and chatting. Everyone was having a good time. They were telling stories about Mr. Fine's last two book signing events. Some fans were in NY and at both events.

Sara recognized many fans. Fans were happy to see her from the Facebook page. Many complimented Sara on her photos and thanked her for her photos.

Mrs. Fine went to every table again to see if fans are eating and continued to watch over fans. Then she sat down to grab her dinner and Mr. Fine came up from behind.

Mr. Fine's fan clapped and everyone grabbed their cameras. Some were hitting their wine glasses for Mr. Fine to kiss Mrs. Fine and playing around. Others were filming and taking pictures. After Mr. Fine walked in, he walked towards Mrs. Fine. And stopped! He looked up at the fans and said:

Mr. Fine: "Every time I do this I usually blackout!"

Fan 1: Yelled: "Someone get a pillow so he doesn't hurt himself on the floor! "Then Mr. Fine bends over to Mrs. Fine tilting his head . . .

Mr. Fine: I love you Darling!

Mrs. Fine: I love you even more and tilts her head to kiss Mr. Fine.

Mr. Fine: Kissed Mrs. Fine real gentle and romantically on the lips and it lasted about several minutes.

Fans went wild. Many hormones were raging in the back room and vibes were high. Everyone laughed and was having so much fun. Many had to use the bathroom after Mr. Fine was done kissing Mrs. Fine because everyone was laughing so hard.

Mr. Fine: He walked away and stopped at Sara's table and cracked a few jokes. The fans were laughing as he exited the back room to say hello to fans. Mrs. Fine went from table to table to chat with fans and get to know fans.

Mr. Fine walked out the room to grab his dinner. Mr. Fine said hello to many of his fans who he saw in NYC. Mr. Fine quickly grabbed something from the buffet table and came back down to sit next to Mrs. Fine. He finally ate his dinner. Mr. Fine ate barbeque chicken, potato, and green beans. Mrs. Fine had a salad.

Some fans did group photos with Mr. Fine. Other fans wanted individual photos. Mr. Fine went to every table to chat with fans. He took some personal time to talk to them and had stories to share with each fan. He also thanked each fan again for coming, saying how nice it is to have such loyalty in our group.

One fan asked a question on that obnoxious fan at Sara's table. Sara got up and walked way and said she needed to use the bathroom. Mr. Fine watched Sara leave. He wondered if Sara saw Roy before the dinner party at the bar. She made sure she wasn't seen. She walked back in quietly. She sat down by Mr. Fine.

Mr. Fine: Everything okay Sara?

Sara: I'm fine Mr. Fine? Just don't feel well.

Mr. Fine: I hope you're feeling better Sara, your awfully quiet. (Mr. Fine still wondered if Sara saw Roy).

Sara: I think I'm okay Mr. Fine. Just a bit tired from travelling. It's a long first day.

Mr. Fine: I hear you Sara. I know what you mean. I'm feeling that tonight. Did you fly here?

Sara: No, I took the train here with my cousin. It was a long ride.

Mr. Fine: I flew from California and was up early this morning.

Sara: Me too. I mean, I was up early. But I kind of relaxed on the train. But the scenery was so pretty with those quaint historical stores and boutiques. The scenery with the leaves changing colors is so very pretty I wanted to stop and go shopping. I thought about asking my cousin to shop but he had business to do in his room and I only had forty minutes to shop. I knew my answer was no.

Mr. Fine: Mrs. Fine wanted to do the same thing but I had to be signing autographs. She wanted to go shopping in the boutiques and see the historical side streets, but I told her no. You and Mrs. Fine would get along great. I have to introduce you to her.

Sara: I met your wife. She so gorgeous I can't believe how pretty and smart she is.

Mr. Fine: How long are you staying.

Sara: Sunday morning. I have to work Monday.

Mr. Fine: What do you do for a living?

Sara: I'm a security greeter Mr. Fine. I do security and run the front desk at a high school. I watch security cameras and keep schools safe. It's a god job!

Mr. Fine didn't know Sara just told a fib and is also on disability. (She is physically disabled and injured her low back. She is trying to get off of disability).

Mr. Fine: (Got up). Well Sara it was wonderful talking to you and everyone at this table. I have to see what my wife is doing and then go sit at another table.

Sara: Thank you Mr. Fine it was great talking to you.

Mindy asked Sara if she was okay. Mr. Fine turned around and Sara saw that Sara was looking annoyed and notice something upset her. Mr. Fine went to sit with Mrs. Fine. It was getting pretty late and people were getting tipsy but having a wonderful evening.

Mrs. Fine: (looks and nods at Sara but whispers) Is everything okay with Sara?? She Seemed upset when she came back in.

Richard: I'm not sure. That guy was at the bar. I'm wondering if Sara knows him. He was at LC in NYC last week and acting obnoxious. Sara made a wise crack about him and I laughed. I'm concerned about her.

Mrs. Fine: hymm. Very smart..Yep! I don't know her very well but I notice that. We have to keep an eye out for her just in case and an eye on her.

Sara stares at Mrs. and Mr. Fine. She's wondering if they are talking about her Sara was wondering if they figured out, she saw Roy. Mindy turned to Sara and asked what was wrong.

Sara knocked over the glass with water by accident and they both started to laugh Mr. Fine turned to look at Sara and wondered what was up with her!

Richard: Yes, we have to keep an eye on her I have a feeling she is fibbing about our friend. (He handsomely leans forward to kiss Leena talking about Sara). I wonder what she is hiding. (He whispers hot and sexy in Leena's ear), and he gives Leena another kiss on the lips. The wine glasses went off.

Richard: Turns around and cracks a joke. It's very hard having a sex symbol for a wife and distracting. I honestly can't concentrate in public when she's around. I mean I need a large dosage of Ritalin whenever she's around.

All the fans crack up with laughter. It continued for a while. The group decided to do a group photo for Mr. and Mrs. Fine. They decided to give it to them as a big thank you for inviting them out. It was getting pretty late. Sara finally got most of the girls together for a group photo. The other table was having a great time and wanted to continue to chat with Mr. and Mrs. Fine. At end of the evening everyone wished each other well. They said we'd see each other on the lines for autograph signings. Also, The Fines be interviewed by a radio host for a local radio station.

Chapter 13

The Obsession

The next morning was Friday. Sara woke up and woke up Mindy to let her know she would be going to the gym and café. If she wanted to meet her in about an hour to text her. So, Mindy said she would. Robert was up and texted Sara to see if she wanted to go to the café and Sara said yes.

The hotel was very quiet and not busy with people at seven o'clock in the morning. Sara checked her phone and Mindy said she would be there and give her a little over an hour. She went to the gym and did the treadmill for forty minutes and then did some stretching.

Then when she was finished, she met Robert at the café. Robert already had coffee he had an egg sandwich. Sara got a granola parfait. The café was very small. It had delicious food, great coffee set up for customers and guests. Sara paid for her breakfast and sat down with Robert.

Robert: So, what are your plans today??

Sara: Well at 9 a.m., which is about an hour I plan on going downstairs and seeing Mr. and Mrs. Fine. I want to do some photo shots with them. I plan on getting that done with them. I would like a professional shot with Mr. and Mrs. Fine. I'm so excited. Do you want to do professional shots with them?

Robert: Yes. I will be doing that and I will go down with you. I like Rachael Goldstein and want a professional shot with her.

Sara: Cool. I am getting my picture with her too. I saw that guy last night at the bar.

Robert: Really? What was he doing?

Sara: He looked like he was going to harass Mr. Fine. He was sitting outside the restaurant.

Robert: He's really creepy.

Sara: Yeah, I know what you mean. I went to the bathroom and came back quickly because he was standing outside and I didn't want to tell Mr. Fine.

(Mrs. Fine walks in the café and heard what Sara said).

Sara: Hi Mrs. Fine. (Sara kicked Robert).

Mrs. Fine: Hi Sara how are you. Are you coming down for autographs in a few minutes?

Sara: Yes, I am. This is my cousin Robert.

Mrs. Fine: (Shakes hands with Robert). Hi Robert. Nice to meet you.

Robert: Nice to meet you. I'm a big fan of You and Racheal Goldstein. Two gorgeous ladies and very good actresses.

Mrs. Fine: (So flattering) Why thank you Robert. I hope to see you downstairs.

Robert: Yes, you will. I am doing professional shots with you and Mr. Fine.

Mrs. Fine: Great and will I see you Sara?

Sara: Yes Mrs. Fine. (Sara hesitates) . . . Mrs. Fine? (she hesitates again).

Mrs. Fine: What is it hun?

Sara: Nothing. I like your blue shirt.

Mrs. Fine: Thank you Sara. I will see you downstairs in a bit. Mrs. Fine goes to the counter and grabs two cups of coffee, coffee tray and two muffins. She then pays for it. She takes in downstairs to the autograph signing room. Sara looked up at her and smiled with sense of guilt because she knew she didn't tell the whole truth about some stuff. Sara then turned and she saw reporters coming in. They were coming in with cameras and microphones. They were following Mrs. Fine and Rachael Goldstein.

Mr. Fine followed both Mrs. Fine and Rachael Goldstein. . Also, a few more celebrities from Riker's Hospital came which Mr. Fine looked surprised. Robert took out his camera and got A few photos of Mr. Fine. He took photos of the cast from Riker's Hospital. Mindy walked in right after they left. She grabbed an egg sandwich. She sat at the table with Robert and Sara.

Mindy: What time does the autograph show start Sara?

Sara: In about a half hour. Mindy, this is Robert.

Mindy: Hi Robert nice to meet you. I know it was kind of busy yesterday and crazy.

Robert: Yes. I had work to catch up for my business.

Mindy: Oh! what kind of business do you do.

Robert: I'm a freelance photographer for many celebrities.

Mindy: Wow! Does Mr. Fine know?

Robert: I think so. I take many photos of celebrities and celebs contact me for

their pictures. I make the glossy photos for the stars. So, when fans like you come in and see the photos that's what I do.

Mindy: Cool. Does it pay well?

Robert: Yes. I get like $100 per photo. So, if I sell photos in a week, I make like $1,000 a week at times.

Mindy: Wow! What time should we be going down?

Sara: I don't know I'd say in about fifteen minutes. They just walked by.

Robert: Yeah. There are probably fans downstairs.

Mindy, Sara, and Robert waited about several minutes then they went downstairs into the convention room where the celebrities from Riker's Hospital were greeting fans.

Mindy, Sara, and Robert went downstairs to get their picture done with celebrities from Riker's Hospital. When they got downstairs, fans and celebs were talking to reporters. They were getting set up to greet their fans. Sara went first to take her picture with Jim Rod from Riker's Hospital. He was in a separate room from the Fines. Mindy held Sara's spot in line and she went over to Jim Rod's line to wait for a photo. When she was online, she notices Roy but wasn't sure because he was talking to some girl and threw Sara off. Sara didn't say anything but she just watched. After Sara took her picture, she thanked Jim Rod for taking the photo. Sara walked away and watched Roy. Roy stepped up to Jim Rod.

Roy: Hey sir, where ja get ya tie. From Mr. Fine?? Looks like his dog ate yours too!!

Sara: (turns around and looks at Roy).

Jim Rod: Sir if your going to get a picture please let another fan go ahead of you.

Roy: How was Mrs. Fine on the set of Riker's Hospital? Was she on the Set? I'm Curious? Was she a good kisser or did she need practice? Did her husband Richard teach her how to kiss right or did she need extra tutoring on the side? I have a card to give you to give to Mrs. Fine if she wants to come back to the set. I will be more than happy to train her in smooching on the set. The thing is I would have to be her partner.

Jim Rod: (turns to security) Security remove this fan please. *Security came by..and Roy looked at the bouncer.*

Roy: I was just having fun and play acting. God can't you take a joke? Roy left and went to the other room where Racheal Goldstein was and the Fines were. Jim Rod sat down and needed a minute. Then he allowed fans to come up to his desk and say hello. Sara grabbed her camera real fast and took a picture.

After Sara took her picture with Jim Rod she went into the room where Mr. and Mrs Fine were. The lines looked longer but Sara went to wait online for Mr. and Mrs. Fine. She wanted to first get a photo sitting in between them. Then she wanted a professional shot with the Fines in the private photo booth.

When Sara went inside the other room the lines were huge. The security guards used two chairs to block fans from coming through. Mr. and Mrs. Fine were being interviewed before allowing fans through to sign autographs. Interviews were rather private. Sara thought and wondered why they were taped, but not taped live. Fans were waiting to see Mr. and Mrs. Fine.

They were also waiting to see the stars of Riker's Hospital. Sara was so excited. She didn't understand why there was a hold up and the lines were so long. Roy apparently was already inside she figured he was probably there. Meanwhile, across from the Fines, Roy pays a visit to Rachael Goldstein on Riker's Hospital.

Roy: Walks up to Rachael and her body guard Phil. I'm interested in this photo.

Rachael: (pointing to Roy's request). This one she says?

Roy: No, this one pretty baby?

Rachael: Looks down and points and is about to grab it as Roy jerks her around.

Roy: As a matter of speaking it's this one. (he points to the other photo). *Phil is playing with his phone.* Hey! Hey! good looking whatcha got cooking? I like you better in that black outfit with the hooks. You know, that picture that's above you. Mighty sexy in that one. How's about getting changed in it over at my place. Maybe your hooks can hook up to my belt and we can disconnect them at my place.

Racheal: (nudges Phil to get off the phone).

Phil:(took a few seconds then hung up his phone).

Mr. Fine was signing autographs. Mrs. Fine looked up and wanted to yell at Roy. She nudged Richard. Mrs. Fine stood up to yell. Phil was going from table to table make sure everyone was okay.

Richard: Sit down darling.

Leena: Darling he's harassing you.

Richard: (signing autographs). I know ignore him and sit down.

Security Guard 1: Is there something wrong Mrs. Fine?

Mrs. Fine: Yes. That man is mocking us and my husband. He tried to pick me up at the bar last Night.

Security Guard 1: How about I sit here and we just hold up the line for a few minutes until this guy leaves. So, the security guard sat in between Mr. and Mrs. Fine to make sure they were safe. Mr. Fine was really happy and gave Roy a look so did the security guard.

Rachael (stood up and moved to the other side, she was getting annoyed).

Phil: Got up and walked over to Roy. He put his right thumb up and pointed it behind him and said: "Take a hike Mike!"

Roy: My name aint Mike Pike!

Security Guard 2: Is there a problem here.

Roy: No, I was just leaving.

Phil: He needs to leave.

Roy: I said I was going.

Roy: The same thing I said to Rachael goes to you babe!

Rachael: Looked away and greeted other fans. Security came by to start to escort Roy away.

Roy: Turns to the security guard. Oh! I forgot. I left my wallet on the table back there.

Security guard #2: Go really fast. I'm watching right here. If you're not back in five minutes I'm escorting you out.

Roy walks back towards where Mr. and Mrs. Fine were. Mr. and Mrs. Fine were about to take a picture with four fans named Angel. Roy walked up to them and started singing. "Angels We Have Heard on High."

Mrs. Fine: Hello girls. What's your name?

Angel #1: (with the blonde hair and glasses) Our name is Angel.

Mrs. Fine: Four Angels? Robert look they are all named Angel. 1. 2..3. 4 .as Mrs. Fine was counting.

Roy: Hello Angels, I'm Charlie.

Angels: Just stare at Roy.

Richard: (turns to Roy) Take a hike pal. What can I do for you lovely ladies?

Angel #2: With the red hair. We would like a picture with you.

Richard: Sure. Richard takes a picture with the four Angels.

Roy: Hello Angels.

Angel #3: (blonde hair) Turn to each other. Who the hell is that!

Angel#4: (brown hair) I don't know.

Mr. Fine: Just ignore him. He's been bullying all morning and is being escorted out in about two seconds. *Mr. Fine shouts* Can I have a security guard please?

Security Guard #2: Security knew exactly who to come for and escorted Roy out the door.

Sara was quietly filming Roy and was up next and knew that something was up. As soon as security went for Roy, she filmed it and shut her camera off. After the four angels had their picture taken with Mr. Fine. Sara was up next.

Sara: Hello Mr. Fine.

Mr. Fine: Hello Sara. Darling (turns to Leena) Sara's here!

Mrs. Fine: Hello Sara..

Sara: Hello Mrs. Fine.

Mrs. Fine: What can we do for you Sara?

Sara: Can I have a picture with you and Mr. Fine in the Photo Booth?

Mr. Fine: Sure, a professional one?

Sara: Yes.

Mrs. Fine: Sure.

Mr. Fine: Yes. Mr. Fine got up with Mrs. Fine and walked with Sara in the booth.

Mrs. Fine: (Tried to talk to Sara to see if she knew Roy). Is everything okay Sara?

Sara: Yes. I just think someone was following me but I'm not sure.

Mrs. Fine: What did he look like?

Mr. Fine: Looked at Mrs. Fine.

Sara: Never mind. I'm probably paranoid. (Sara thought Roy might have been outside so she clammed up). It's probably my imagination.

Mrs. Fine: Looks at Mr. Fine.

Mr. Fine: Puts his two arms on Sara's shoulders and whispers in a gentle voice in Sara's ear.

Sara if there's something you need to tell us, now's the time to do it.

Photographer: (interrupts) Are you all doing a photo?

Sara: (responds really fast) Yes. Yes, we are.

Photographer: Please smile for the picture.

Photographer: (smile for the picture) Mr. and Mrs. Fine, and Sara smiled.

Sara: (turned and looked up to Mr. Fine). I would just feel stupid if I am wrong.

Mr. Fine: Don't feel stupid Sara. What is it?

Sara: That guy?

Photographer: Okay we have to move onto the next fan.

Sara: I'm alright Mr. Fine. I think I'm just paranoid. Sara clams up and decides not to tell Mr. Fine.

Mr. Fine: Will I see you tonight at the news interview?

Sara: Yes Mr. Fine I will see you tonight.

Mrs. Fine: Okay Sara. See you then.

Mr. and Mrs. Fine and Sara walk out into the room with fans. Roy has apparently left and is nowhere to be seen.

Chapter 14

Mr. Fine's Plea

Mr. and Mrs. Fine just got done finishing up last minute autographs with fans before heading towards their interview. They both got changed and freshened up. No one knew what the interview was about except for Mr. and Mrs. Fine. Mr. and Mrs. Fine decided to do an interview for Mr. Fine's book and then they thought about doing a news story their daughter's disappearance.

Reporters lined up from outside to watch the interview and ask questions as Mr. Fine was putting the story out there for the public to listen to help find Lynn. Hundreds of fans and public showed up for this event to listen to Mr. Fine put Lynn's missing persons story out there. Many figured he was going to do it.

The same reporters that were outside waited inside patiently waiting to tape Mr. and Mrs. Fine and support anyway they can. After fans got their autograph with Mr. Fine, they went inside to listen to Mr. Fine speak on his book. They knew he would speak out and put the message out there for Lynn's kidnappers. They knew he would be asking for Lynn's safe return to the home

Mr. Fine and Mrs. Fine walked in and sat down with the news person Dave. The audience applauded for several minutes and the Fines waited as the audience calmed down

Mr. Fine: (Puts his hand in the air) Thank you. Thank you so very very much and thank you for coming out to see my wife and I. This is my beautiful wife Leena Fine. Leena turns as she blushes in front of the crowd (the audience whistles really loud). Thank you. This is Dave our announcer. (audience applauds).

The focus goes on to Richard Fine.

Richard Fine: Good Evening! My name is Richard Fine. I live in Los Angeles, California. I am owner of Hotel Chiller in California. I retired awhile back and decided to become an author. I decided write about celebrities in Hollywood California. I wrote a book it is called "I Loved Her in The Eighties." Most of my story focuses on the actors from Riker's Hospital.

Since the majority of the cast was going to be here today, I picked this weekend in particular to do an autograph show for my book. Another reason why I am here tonight is to plea to my daughters' kidnappers, who disappeared a week in a half ago.

Her car was found on the side of the road with her pocketbook wallet in the front seat of the car. The second half of my discussion will be on our daughter Lynn Fine's disappearance and I will give a description to all on what happened.

Dave: Mr. Fine what inspired you to write "I Loved Her in The Eighties"?

Mr. Fine: Like I said Dave. I got my inspiration from my wife Leena being on a daytime drama show Riker's Hospital. She left shortly after Roy Martin attacked her on the set.

Also, I own a a chain of Hotels in California and "Hotel Chiller." My hotel is home to the sets of many movies and television shows. Film and television directors from all over came in and used my hotel for their pictures. I always comped them and they would allow me to photograph actors and actress who came on the set. At times, we got roles as extras and walk ons. They always needed people.

Dave: Mrs. Fine, do you still write for the show? I know you use to write for it as well.

Mrs. Fine: I still write for Riker's Hospital, but I washed my hand of the acting part because of the attack that happened on the set.

Dave: Mr. Fine, do you plan on writing for the show at all or have you ever been approached for writing for Riker's Hospital?

Mr. Fine: I haven't been approached yet. If I do get approached, I would certainly consider it.

Lynn use to love that show. As a matter of speaking she watched that show up to her disappearance. She would have that set turned on from 2:30pm to 3pm week days every day to watch it. She almost had a part on that show as a kid. She had huge gray eyes. That was something producers never saw, and they wanted me to sign her on, but I wouldn't do it.

Mrs. Fine: Lynn and I use to watch it. I miss watching it with her and our time discussing what would happen to the characters. Lynn would give me tips on writing and wanted to be included in writing for Riker's Hospital. I will never forget getting a role on that show back in the day and wanting our daughter to play an actor's illegitimate child.

I am amazed at what they came up with with storylines. I was excited to see many of the actors and actress here today. Many still asking if there was any information on Lynn.

Mr. Fine: Yes. It was nice getting reacquainted with them. I had drinks last night with Rachael Goldstein. Rachael did approach me on wanting me to write. My inspiration started here. I use to photograph the cast of Riker's Hospital. One year back in the eighties when they had a big wedding, our hotel ball room was used as a scene.

In addition, many directors used our hotel for their movie sets because of our design and set up. I was able to photograph celebrities who stopped by. As the years went by, I decided to write on each celebrity I came in contact with. Then, I went to school and got my Masters in English/Writing.

I decided I wanted to publish a book on celebrities and go on autograph signings shows. I wanted to speak on celebrities I met. When I retired part time from the hotel, I decided to write my book. Lynn always encouraged me to write with Riker's Hospital. It was hard not telling her she couldn't have a role. I don't mean to change gears but I would like to speak about Lynn. She was my daughter and my best friend. She always looked out for me. She would even cook and clean. Although we had maids and butlers, I never needed a maid or butler the last seven years, because Lynn was there for Leena and me.

She worked extremely hard at the hotel and always directed guests in a professional manner. She was only twenty-five when she went missing and just had a huge birthday party at the house.

Mrs. Fine: I get sad every time I think about Lynn not being in the kitchen. I miss her not playing with our dogs Scotch and Whisky. Lynn and I would dress them up. Lynn was so funny. One year she found squeaky toys of for Scotch and Whisky. She found squeaky bottles and bought them for the dogs. The dogs were scared of them and Whisky hid them. I miss not watching Riker's Hospital with her and not greeting guests at our hotel. We have a butler and maid but our daughter was also a helper as well.

Over a week ago, Lynn disappeared and her car was found off the side of the road a few miles from the hotel. I was mortified. She left the hotel to go to the store at 3pm but never returned. Lynn was wearing a jacket, blue jeans, red shirt, and short black boots.

(Mrs. Fine holds up a picture was pointing out to the audience). This is a picture of our daughter Lynn Fine. It makes me so angry to think that Lynn could be out there hurt somewhere, or had some type of accident. Her car was found off the side of the road. There was a large blood stain on the driver's seat. There was also blood on the driver's seat and blood on the passenger's seat as well. We weren't sure what happened or if foul play was involved.

Mrs. Fine looked down and thought about what could have happened to Lynn. Lynn was a jokester she said. We thought it was a joke at first. A long time ago she played a joke on us. It took a week to find out what happened to her. She wanted to be unpredictable and disappear for a few days. Last week the joke wasn't a joke anymore.

Richard: We live in Los Angeles: Our Single-Family Home is located at 3099 Mandeville Canyon Rd, Los Angeles, CA. 3099 Mandeville Canyon Rd is in the Brentwood neighborhood in Los Angeles, CA and in ZIP Code 90049. It is approximately 5,930 square feet and was built in 1940.

Lynn was driving a Mercedes Benz.

I am coming here tonight to plea with anyone with information. Please, please call my line at this number on the photo or police tip line in Los Angeles, California. If you see anything, no matter how small the details just let them know. This is the hotline number to Hotel Chiller in Los Angeles.

We are also being taped via satellite and this program will be aired in California and throughout the US. We Have a hotline set up and a person answering it at the desk for any information on Lynn Fine. You can also contact my website at www.richardfineauthor.com or just go to Richard Fine. If you had a loved one loss or missing you would make a plea on television and want closure for that person too. (The news people from Los Angeles shut the tape off).

Camera Man: That's a wrap Mr. Fine.

Mrs. Fine: We will now take questions from the audience.

Fan#1: Any news come in on Lynn's disappearance?

Leena: Not that we are aware of.

Fan #2: (raises hand) Who me?

Mr. Fine: Yes you.

Fan #2: Did anyone ever tell you your wife is a pretty bitch.

Mr. Fine: Excuse me?

Fan #2: Does she think you had anything to do with Lynn's disappearance or situation.

Mr. Fine: I'm not exactly sure I understand that question. Yes you. (Mr. Fine ignores him).

Fan #3: Do they have any leads on Lynn's disappearance?

Mr. Fine: No leads. No leads that foul play is involved. (another fan raises their hand).

Fan #4: Was there any evidence of a car accident.

Mr. Fine: There was some blood found on Lynn's seat and seat on the passenger side. We are still waiting on forensics to see if it's all Lynn's blood. The car wasn't damaged.

Fan #5: Could Lynn have been kidnapped?

Mrs. Fine: We haven't received a ransom call or any calls yet.

Fan #6: Could someone has had a jealousy issue with you or Lynn?

Mr. Fine: That's an avenue that is being explored.

Fan #7: Was Lynn with anyone else at the time or meeting anyone else?

Mrs. Fine: Lynn was shopping at Brentwood Center in Los Angeles near the hotel area.

Fan #8: Did anything strange happen prior to Lynn's disappearance?

Mr. and Mrs. Fine both look at each other with a puzzled look. Mrs. Fine smiled and said: that's a really good thought I haven't thought of that. And turned her head.

Mr. Fine: Thank you so much for listening and Please if anyone knows anything or hears something through social media contact the LA police department.

Dave: That concludes our evening with Mr. Richard and Leena Fine.

The audience applauds and gives a big applaud. Everyone gets up and starts to walk out. Mr. and Mrs. Fine quickly exit and go to the restaurant. Sara, Mindy, Robert, some other fans decide to go to the same restaurant as the night before, to eat dinner and talk about the discussion. They had no clue Mr. and Mrs. Fine would be there.

Sara couldn't believe the same type of questions were being asked and thought it was suspicious that the same question from the atrium center in NYC was asked. So, Sara, Robert, Mindy and a few fans walk in the restaurant.

Sara and Gloria walk in the restaurant. Sara starts mocking one of the commentators. She reacts to his question and mocks Mr. Fine's answer. Gloria is watching and cracking up laughing.

Sara: Mocks one of the fans. "Is your wife a pretty bitch. She held her hand like a microphone and puts her mouth to her hand. Excuse me Mr. Fine, could you tell me if your wife is a pretty bitch?

Gloria: Nudges on Sara. Sara stop turn around. Your caught!

Sara: Turns around and Mr. and Mrs. Fine is behind her smirking at the corner table.

Sara: Yeouch...! Sara laughed. Oh crap! Sara was fooling around laughing.

Mr. Fine: (watching Sara turns to Mrs. Fine) she's hiding something.

Mrs. Fine: Yes, she is. (she gets up and walks out).

Gloria: Laughed again. We need a drink.

Sara, Gloria, Robert and Mindy sat directly across from Mr. and Mrs. Fine. Rachael Goldstein and Jim Rod walked in the restaurant and had dinner with Mr. Fine. Jim Rod came over and said hello to all of us and then had dinner with the Fines. Everyone chatted at the table and had a good time. Mr. and Mrs. Fine knew Sara was hiding something. Sara knew she was caught in a lie about Roy. Sara went up to the Fines and wanted to say good bye. Sara was curious if the Fines knew she lied.

Sara: Walked up to Mr. Fine.

Mr. Fine: Hello Sara.

Sara: Hello Mr. Fine just wanted to say goodbye and safe travels back to Los

Angeles. I am a bit tired and will be going to bed now. I know you will be at Graveyard Theater in a few weeks. I made reservations.

Mr. Fine: You have a safe trip home too Sara. Mrs. Fine isn't here. She's in the bathroom if you want to say goodbye to her.

Sara: Thank you Mr. Fine. I will go see if I can find Mrs. Fine. Sara walks to the bathroom.

Sara didn't want Mrs. Fine knowing she was tired. (So, she came up with a lie. Sara opens the bathroom door and sees Mrs. Fine brushing her beautiful brown straight hair). Hi Mrs. Fine.

Mrs. Fine: Hello Sara, how are you?

Sara: Good. Mr. Fine told me I can find you in here. I wanted to say goodbye to you and wish you safe travels home.

Mrs. Fine: That's so sweet of you. (Mrs. Fine gave Sara a hug).

Sara: I know you and me will be at Graveyard Theater in New Jersey. I will be going back to make reservations now.

Mrs. Fine: Okay Sara. Have a safe trip home.

Sara exits and goes back to the restaurant to tell the others she's' going back to her room in a bit. It just so happened everyone got tired and they all decided to leave the room at once. Mr. and Mrs. Fine walked back to their hotel room. They slowly walked down the long corridor. Mr. Fine put his arms around Mrs. Fine. They went into their state room.

Sara, Mindy and Robert went back to their room. Sara took out her key. She tried to open the door and it did not open. It was getting pretty late. Mindy didn't want to walk down a long dark hallway to the elevator. So, Sara did. Sara walked down the long dark hallway with no one there. Mindy was left alone. Sara went downstairs to exchange keys. Sara went to the front desk. Sara thought someone was following her. But when she got to the desk, she saw Roy lurking around in the dark. Sara saw Roy watching Mr. Fine's room and went to the security guard. Mrs. Fine happened to be in the lobby and saw Sara.

Mrs. Fine: Is everything okay Sara?

Sara: Yes Mrs. Fine. I just got locked out of my room.

Mrs. Fine: The front desk will give you another key Sara?

Sara: Thank you Mrs. Fine. I will get one now. (turns to the security guard) Can you walk me back to my room there's a strange guy down the hallway by Mr. Fine room.

Mrs. Fine: Thank you Sara for saying something. I wouldn't go past there.

Sara: Your welcome Mrs. Fine. I was a bit nervous and don't want to walk alone. You shouldn't walk alone either. There's someone by your door.

Mrs. Fine: I don't blame you. I will wait for security to take me back.

Sara got a new key to the front desk and asked security guard to walk her back to her room. The security guard was well aware Roy was obnoxious and decided to walk Sara back. Sara walked safely back to her room. Mindy and Sara went to bed. They were leaving bright and early to go home the next morning.

Meanwhile, Roy walked back to his room after hanging out by Mr. Fine's door. He took out his cell phone and called the Los Angelo's Police Tip line. He finally gets their answering service and says: "Pretty Bitch and then hangs up." Then he takes out his cell phone and he takes out Mrs. Fine's Photo! (Who Are You Really???)

Photo You will be mine one day Mrs. Fine All Mine!

Chapter 15

Graveyard Theater

A few weeks passed by and it was time to go on another book signing event for Mr. Fine. Sara could hardly wait. Sara couldn't wait to meet up with some of the fans from Mr. Fine's book club. Sara called Robert to see if he can go, but unfortunately Robert started a new job and could not attend Graveyard Theater in Parsipanny, New Jersey for the upcoming weekend.

When Sara first booked the room, all the rooms were taken. Sara had to go to the hotel next door which is connected to Graveyard Hotel. Sara called two days before to confirm reservations. She double checked with the front desk receptionist and was able to get another room in the same hotel. Sara was excited. She was excited to be in the same hotel with Mr. and Mrs. Fine. Jean decided she wanted to go and see Mr. Fine again. Jean decided to meet Sara at the hotel on Saturday.

Sara walked outside her apartment door and waited for the cab. While she waited outside her Lakeview apartment, she started feeding the swans. She stared at the lake feeding the swans. She thought it's the end of October, the lake should be frozen, but it wasn't yet. The cab pulled up to take Sara to the train station.

The station was about twenty minutes away. When she got to the train station, she checked in to see what track she was on.

She looked up to the monitor and read **Track 2 NYC**, highlighted in red. She walked to track two. Then she walked back to the snack bar to grab a couple of snacks to take with her for her ride to New York City. Sara went to the snack bar to grab food to New York City. She decided to have a bagel with butter, water and chips. Then she went to catch her train. She went down a flight of stairs with luggage and all to track two. She looked up on the monitor and saw that the train was on time with no changes for tracks.

The horn got really loud as the train was pulling up towards the track. The wheels were slowing down as the train came to a full stop on the tracks. Sara walked down always until the sliding doors opened.

Then Sara boarded the train. When she got in, she was able to grab the first seat. There were four empty seats. Sara grabbed the first cart. She took out her boarding pass and put it in the front chair.

Conductor: "TRAIN FOR NEW YORK CITY," says the conductor. "HAVE YOUR TICKETS OUT." "TICKETS OUT PLEASE!" the conductor walked down the aisle checking tickets, clicking them and keeping them on the chair.

The train doors closed. The train started to move. Fifteen minutes passed by and Sara took out Mr. Fine's book "I Loved Her in The Eighties." She figured she could at least get a chapter read in the hour in a half she had to travel. She was on the third chapter where Roy Martin was attacking Mrs. Fine in the studio. As she came to the end of the chapter the train was ready to stop.

What a long chapter she thought as she shut the book and organized her bag. She just starred at the handsome penmanship Mr. Fine had when she was shutting her book. She grabbed everything she needed and made sure her stuff was put away in her bags.

Conductor: "NYC" NYC the conductor announced. Next stop "NEW YORK CITY."

Once the train stopped Sara got out and went to the next gate to where the second train was leaving for Graveyard Theater in New Jersey. She had looked up at the monitor to get her gate number, and sat out by her gate for a little bit. Sara sat and watched travelers. So busy she thought, shuffling and hustling to their buses. Travelers were looking up at the monitors for their track numbers.

People were up and down the escalators. Sara watched others going to the different snack bars and shopping stores. There was a lot of traffic and there was a lot of energy travelling going on at Penn Station. Police and security guards were stationed at every corner. There was even a police station at the corner where Sara's gate was. One corner had one handsome military man and two handsome police officers.

She thought to herself, I better pay attention to the time instead of these officers or I will miss my train to Graveyard Theater. Sara started daydreaming and starring at the officers again. Jean texted her and asked her where she was? Then asked her what she was doing? Sara texted back and said she was in New York City waiting for the next train to Parsipanny, New Jersey. Plus, she texts" I am starring at three good looking men in uniform." Jean sent a laughing message back to Sara.

Sara: texted "My bus leaves in about a half hour." "I'm at the gate."

Sara texted again: There's more good-looking men in uniform. I may have to miss my bus and search for them."

Jean: Texts back" you're crazy.

Sara: Should be at Graveyard Theater by 2pm.

"Chat with you when I am checked in." Sara shut her phone. It was getting closer to Parsippany Train station. Sara tried several times to call for transportation from the theater to Graveyard Hotel. She had no luck calling for transportation. When the train arrived, Sara got off and put her bags on the bench outside on the walkway of the tracks. She looked up and saw a van labeled Graveyard Theater.

Sara: Going to the Graveyard Theater? You Hoo! (Sara Is Waving).

Sara: Driver? Driver? Are you going to Graveyard Theater?

Driver: Yes. Yes, I am. Want a lift?

Sara: Yes! How much?

Driver: Ten dollars.

Sara: (Sara was excited and she walked fast down the grassy, rocky hill to the parking lot where the shuttle was picking up passengers). Sara paid the driver.

Thank You so much.

Driver: Get in.

Sara: (Hops into the van) This is great.

Driver: *Takes Sara's bag and puts them in the Graveyard Theater Van. Then he goes and sits in the van.* Okay I think that's it. We are full and ready to roll. The mini Graveyard Theater Van fit six passengers. Sara got the last seat and front seat.

Sara: Thank you, so much. I didn't know what I was going to do.

Driver: We are glad to help you.

Sara: I saw you on the web and tried several times to call but couldn't get an answer, but I'm glad you waited here.

Driver: Yes, our website was down for some reason. People couldn't get through. I'm glad we have a full van. I waited her because I knew the website was down.

Driver: *Takes off to Graveyard Theater.* Where are you from?

Sara: Poughkeepsie, New York. Where are you from?

Driver: I live here in the town of Parsippany, New Jersey.

Sara: So, you must see a lot of places and know where everything is.

Driver: Yes, I do.

Sara: I'm here on a book signing autograph show at Graveyard Theater.

Driver: For who?

Sara: Richard Fine's, "I Loved Her in The Eighties."

Driver: The one whose daughter disappeared from Hotel Chiller?

Sara: Yes.

Driver: I saw the news on that. They broadcasted that on every news station via satellite. Sad the daughter disappeared. I'm wondering if she's not kidnapped or hurt. Sounds like there could be a chance she's still alive and might have had an accident.

Sara: Yes. I pray for a safe return with him or to find out what happened for closure for the Fines. I met the Fines for the first time a few weeks ago and dinner with them. They ate with their fans two weeks ago and had a dinner party. We had so much fun. They treated us very good.

Passenger#1: I was at Mr. Fine's book signing in Baltimore, Maryland last month and was at the Fine's Plea for their daughters return.

Sara: So was I. Where were you sitting.

Passenger #1: I was sitting right up front where Mrs. Fine was speaking on Mr. Fine's side. Do you think anyone came forward regarding his daughter's disappearance?

Sara: I don't know. He has a Facebook page for his group. I was on it but I did not see any new information posted or hear anything in the news. But I'm going to ask Mr. Fine. I will see him in a few hours. I won't be able to see him until 6 or 7 pm tonight.

Driver: He should do another panel discussion at the hotel.

Sara: I didn't see one listed or another interview listed. I think Mr. Fine is just signing autographs.

Driver: Is Mrs. Fine still on that Soap Opera Rikers's Hospital?

Sara: No. But she does write for the show. I think Mr. Fine was approached in Baltimore to write by Rachael Goldstein.

Driver: Yeah. She's hot.

Sara: Laughed.

Driver: So is Mr. Fine's wife.

Sara: (Laughed). Well so is Mr. Fine He's really good looking. I can't concentrate when I'm near him.

Passengers: (Laughing and having fun). Neither can some of us.

Sara: I have a question. Is a fib a lie? Or is it a small lie? (she engages passengers to answer). Then Sara decides to record it on her cell for for Robert to listen to prove him wrong one more time.

Driver: (Laughed chuckled) a fib to me is a lie.

Passenger 1: It all depends (laughs) what would be the fib?

Sara: Well at the Revue in Long Island I took a sneaky side photo of Mr. Fine. I told Mr. Fine I needed pictures of him. But didn't tell him I got sneaky and took a sneaky photo when I wasn't supposed to.

Passenger 1: That would be a lie.

Passenger 2: (laughed) I think it's a fib because you didn't say you didn't have any pictures of him.

Sara suddenly shuts her phone knowing she wouldn't win the conversation with Robert and deletes the conversation.

Passenger 3: Its definitely sneaky. (he laughed.)

Driver: I have to sit on that one, and then laughs. The driver pulls up to the hotel.

Sara: Will you be able to take me back to the train station Sunday.

Driver: Yes. Just give me your number. As for the other passengers who need rides give me your number and I will come and get you.

Passengers: Gave the driver their number and put the drivers number in their contacts. Then went to the hotel.

Sara tipped the driver and checked in at the front desk of the hotel. Her room was available. Sara was able to go to her room right away and see some parts of the hotel of Graveyard Theater. The concierge service attendant took Sara's luggage to her room. The lobby of the hotel was beautiful. It was so pretty. When you first walked in there were large pink quartz objects designed like bracelets hanging down from the ceiling and a high-rise ceiling. It was almost similar to a design back in Baltimore but larger objects. Their high rised ceiling had rectangular windows as well.

There was a luggage closet across the way to hold guest's luggage and a lounge in the front when you walk in. Then there was a Steak House restaurant and a bar down away. Along the side of Graveyard Theater, there were venders with pictures of actors from horror movies. There were celebrity memorabilia's and many other little areas set up as shops. When you walked in some celebrities were stationed up front, while others were in another room.

People were busy setting up their displays and vendors for fans. The hotel was very busy. Many guests were already browsing through some of the vendors. Some wanted to go the autograph shows to see Mr. Fine and other celebrities. The other half of the cast of Rikers's Hospital was going to be there and set up in the front area, where guests walk in.

None of the celebrities were at their tables. The show didn't start until two more hours. Sara was on her way to the elevator and she saw Mr. Fine. He was just coming in and he looked busy. She didn't want to bother him so she took a photo of him. It was hard to get a photo of Mr. Fine. So many fans wanted to talk to him. He looked so handsome in his tie as he was chatting with fans. Sara was amazed with the patience Mr. Fine had with people.

Shortly after Sara took a photo of Mr. Fine, Sara saw the double elevator doors. She put her camera in her pocket. When she looked up, she thought she

saw Roy in the elevator and wearing denim jeans and a jacket and the elevator going down. She wasn't sure and just stared until the elevator door shut. Sara turned to look to see if Mr. Fine was still around but apparently, he left.

Sara started becoming suspicious that Mr. Fine was being followed. She said to herself the next time I see him or if I see him around, I will take a picture. Sara hit the up arrow on the elevator doors and the light came up. A few minutes later the elevator doors opened. Sara got in and hit the sixth floor. When the elevator doors opened, Sara went to her room. She walked out, walked straight ahead and her room was the first room on the right.

Number 656 When she walked in there were two queen beds to the left. It looked so comfortable that Sara wanted to jump in bed and get ready for a nap. She knew she needed to at least take another shower before that. The bathroom was marble with granite counters with two sinks and a large sliding mirror. There was a large bathtub and shower.

In between the double beds, there was two wall lamps. There was a small refrigerator, coffee maker and large television. The room was very large and spacious. Sara unpacked some things, and then turned on the television. She was ready for a nap from a long day's travel. She took a nap for two hours. She knew she be seeing Mr. Fine real soon.

Meanwhile in room 666, Roy was taken out Mrs. Fine's picture. Roy started unpacking his clothes and his dry erase board from his suitcase. Roy knew he had some time and went over a game plan to torment Mr. Fine a little bit longer. He was debating if he was going to kill him in the hotel over the weekend. When he looked at his last ideas, he thought It wasn't horrifying enough so he decided to come up with a new set of ideas. Roy sat on the bed and listed five more ideas.

One idea was to call up every room in the hotel and hand up (prank Calls),

to torment Mr. Fine's fans and fans of Riker's Hospital online.

Roy: What am I going to do next he exclaimed! I have to figure this out. (talking out loud)

He kept the bomb scare threat because he wanted to frighten everyone. Four leave notes underneath all the door and terrorize the hotel guest. Then he thought about going to the copy machine and making copies of Mr. Fine's picture and slashing it and putting in underneath all the fans doors. Roy knew he had a busy weekend. Roy called the front desk.

Roy: Yes, how do I dial into another room and do you have an office to make copies?

Receptionist: You need to dial just the room number and the person should pick up. Copies can be made here or next door at the hotel.

Roy: Okay. Thank you very much. After he hangs up, he says, Thanks Bitch! You will be scared too. Roy tested the receptionist out and dialed his two friends up on the other floor. He called Mary and Cindy. He said he would meet them outside of Graveyard Theater by the ticket entrance for the show in about an hour. When Roy was done, he took out the floor plan to see how many rooms floors there were. Roy dialed each room up.

He let it ring several times until someone answers. He got a little annoyed cause it took about an hour. He wanted to spend time staring and kissing Mrs. Fine's picture. He was confused and in deep thought. He even thought well, maybe I should kidnap her and bring her back to my room for fun. But he didn't have time for that. Not yet anyway. He finally finished calling all the rooms. Then he took out Mr. and Mrs. Fine's picture.

Roy: (talking to himself out loud) What are you doing with him when you can have me? I honestly don't know what you see in him Leena but we have to get this right and straighten things out. You can't have us both so make up your mind!

Roy put these two pictures aside and took out single photos of Mrs. Fine.

When Mr. Fine is gone, we will be together. He starts kissing her photo.

My first present to you is going to be a skirt with some hooks on it. I will by a matching outfit with hooks and we can get hooked up!

Then Roy had to figure out what photo was going to go underneath all the

room doors. He wrote on Leena's lips and then kissed them. On this photo he wrote I love you. Roy took out this photo of Mr. Fine because it pissed him off when he got interviewed with Leena Fine. He decided this would be the better photo. He took it out and put it aside. He wrote on it Richard Fine. Roy wrote a poem behind Mr. Fine's Photo in red and blue.

Roses are Red Violets are blue

Do You know where Lynn is

Maybe I do!

Chapter 16

Richard's Angels

Roy put the picture aside and got ready to go downstairs to wait online with the crowd. It was almost time for the autograph show to open. Roy went down a little bit early to see where Mr. Fine's room could be or get an idea of where his room would be if he was observing. He didn't have to spend as much moneymaking copies, but tormenting Mr. Fine was becoming expensive. Roy talked to himself: Kiss yourself on your brain Roy this will work.

Roy decided to grab his pocketknife and some other things to put in his backpack. Roy went downstairs and walked around the area for a bit to see where Mr. Fine was coming from. Sara left as well and went downstairs to walk around. She just missed Roy. Then, Sara went online and waited for about fifteen minutes. Roy didn't see Mr. Fine, but met up with Cindy and Mary.

Sara went outside. She got in line behind Roy. She looked at him but couldn't tell if it was the guy who caused chaos in NYC. She thought about taking pictures of him and sending him to Robert while she was waiting for him to turn around. At first no one was around. and then Mr. Fine's fans, and fans of Riker's Hospital started lining up at the doors.

Fans started lining up and it got crowded fast. It was almost five and time for the pre-show to open. Security guards were dressed in costumes as knights guarding the doors play acting and keeping fans in line. While standing at the door Sara was taking pictures. Sara had her camera in her hand. Then she put it in her purse. The knight allowed the pre-autograph show to go online first to buy tickets. The six o'clock show line was pretty small. Not many people were on line waiting because everyone moved over to the preshow.

Roy started making comments and threats towards Mr. Fine and Sara watched him.

Roy: I can't wait to get a whole of Mr. Fine and tell him how I feel shouted Roy. (Roy turns for a second towards Sara). Did you kill your daughter Lynn?? Roy Shouts? What did you do? Did you throw her in the Ravine or River?? Did You Strangle Her and Burry Her? Or did you kidnap her and tie her up somewhere and try to blame it on someone else? Or, did you drug her and throw her over the San Francisco Bridge? Maybe you buried her outside your backyard and drove her car to Brentwood. What did you do Mr. Fine? I can't wait to plant evidence at your house and frame you.

I can't wait to tell him and harass him when I see him. I just can't wait to feel up Mrs. Fine's waist, or tickle her by her breast. So, when Mrs. Fine gets angry. I will put my hand on her breast to grab it. She's so pretty when she gets angry, that really turns me on. Cindy and Mary started laughing. Sara got nervous and took out her camera.

Sara snapped a picture of Roy. Roy didn't know. Sara made believe she was a tourist. She went around clicking pictures of the crowd to give the information to Mr. Fine. She decided to sneak off the line before Roy figured out, she was taking photos. Then, she snuck on the 5pm line online to the pre-show to warn Mr. Fine and Mr. Fine's security guard.

Sara got online but the lines were really long inside Graveyard Theater. She was very anxious that Roy was going to do something to Mr. Fine She saw Roy had a backpack. Sara didn't know what was inside or what Roy was bringing into the autograph signing room. Sara went online. She looked up and down to see how long the line was.

Sara saw Angel from the last autograph signing event.

So, she asked a lady to hold her place and walked up to Angel to say hello. When she approached Angel, the other Angels were there and Sara told Angel what had happened. Angels got mad and said report that to the security guard because he doesn't deserve it. Sara told them she thought it was the same person back in Baltimore but cannot be sure because she took a picture of his back. Sara thanked all four angels and went to the security guard.

Sara: Security guard, I heard Mr. Fine being threatened on the line. There's a person outside of Graveyard Theater vocalizing to harass Mr. and Mrs. Fine. As a matter of speaking he vocalized that once Mrs. Fine got angry, he was going to touch her breast and grab it. I also took a photo of him and photographed his back.

I was so very nervous. I didn't know what to do. He stated that he was going to ask Mr. Fine if he killed his daughter and threw her off the bridge in San Francisco.

Security Guard: I need to see the photo. (Sara took out her camera again and showed the security guard his picture) Okay, thank you very much. We are definitely going to watch him.

Security Guard: Someone has been harassing Mr. Fine we need to know who he is. I will look out for him and tell the other security people. Thank you for reporting him. Sara walked back to her line and got online to wait to see Mr. Fine. Sara went back to her line. She thanked the other fan for holding her spot and told her what happened.

Fan: You did the right thing by reporting it to security guard.

Sara: I know. He was really really creepy. What's your name? I'm Sara.

Fan: I'm Lisa.

Sara: Thanks so much for holding my line. Are you a part of the Facebook group? I don't recall see a Lisa listed.

Lisa: No. I just joined today and they let me in. I'm a big fan of Riker's Hospital. I watched Mrs. Fine on Riker's Hospital.

Sara: Yeah me too. Those were the days on Riker's Hospital back in the 80's.

Lisa: You remember that big murder.

Sara: Yes. I cannot believe Roy Martin attacked Mrs. Fine on the set.

Lisa: I know. That was creepy in itself.

Lisa and Sara talked for fifteen minutes online and a half hour passed by. The security guards stopped the line and asked everyone to stay against the wall so celebrities can walk through.

Mr. and Mrs. Fine were doing a photo op in a second room. They were going upstairs to take professional pictures with fans for about an hour. So, it was another long wait. Sara was getting anxious. Then Sara came face to face with Roy online yet once more. Roy was weaving in and out of the hallway taking different entrance ways. He was looking like he was going to do something.

Sara: CRAP!

Lisa: What's wrong?

Sara: I just reported that guy that is circulating around us.

Lisa: Warn security again. He looks creepy.

Sara: I know.

Security Guard: The security guard walked down the aisle one more time to make sure fans were lined up closer to the wall then he came down towards Sara. The security guard was very tall and weighed 180 pounds and looked like age thirty. He was very muscular.

Sara: Excuse Me. Excuse Me sir!

Security: What is it?

Sara: Well!!

Security: Make it fast.

Sara: There is this guy that was outside. He was making threats towards Mr. Fine and Mrs. Fine.

Security: We know all about him.

Sara: He just came in here he is circulating the area.

Security: Were you the one who reported him?

Sara: Yes. I even took a picture.

Security: Let me see what he looks like.

Sara: (took out her camera and showed the security man the photo).

Security: The celebrities know all about it. Don't worry, because he will be walking in with me and attached to me. He won't do anything to Mr. and Mrs. Fine. I will be standing with him.

Sara: Thank you.

Security: Okay. You see him again come up and let us know.

Sara: Okay. He was in and out of this room. He came in and left.

Security: Okay, I will let them know.

Security kept the celebrities inside the room for safety reasons until they felt the halls were clear. Mr. and Mrs. Fine came out. Mr. Fine was gone for about an hour as fans waited for him to come back. It was very very crazy.

Everyone seemed calm and chatting about storylines for Riker's Hospital. Mrs. Fine came out to greet the fans and asked if anyone wanted to come inside and see her. No one responded. Sara clammed up and turned away because she became frightened from seeing. Mrs. Fine went back down and up one more time. At times she did stop and keep fans entertained out in the hall with security watching. Other fans were called in to see other celebrities from Riker's Hospital. The lines were going down and getting smaller. An hour passed by, and Mr. Fine finally returned to the autograph show and everyone clapped.

Sara finally got a chance to walk up again and see Mr. Fine.

Sara: Hello Mr. Fine.

Mr. Fine: Hello Sara. Ready for autograph or picture?

Sara: (smiled) Yes autograph. This was the picture I took in Baltimore of you and Mrs. Fine kissing at our dinner.

Mr. Fine: Sweet. She chatted for a few minutes with Mr. Fine.

Mr. Fine: That is a great photo of Me and Mrs. Fine you took at the Convention.

Show Mrs. Fine She will love it. How long are you staying for Sara?

Sara: Thank you Mr. Fine. I'm staying until Sunday Mr. Fine (Mrs. Fine stared at Sara.

Sara started feeling guilty and made a face. She felt guilty about lying to Mrs. Fine out in the hall. She needed to come up with a quick lie.

Mr. Fine: Is everything okay Sara?

Sara: Yes Mr. Fine. I'm just a bit tired. I travelled all afternoon. Is Marie St. John Here?

Mr. Fine: Yes. She is over there.

Sara: I may want my picture with her too. Can I have my picture with Mrs. Fine too? (Sara knew she'd get caught in a lie but wanted her picture anyway. She came up with a fast excuse and lied about why she said no in the hallway. She knew she didn't want to see Roy again). I will see you tomorrow afternoon in the photo op room.

Mr. Fine: Sure, you can. Leena? Darling?

Leena: What is it darling?

Sara: Sara would like to take a picture with you.

Leena: Hi Sara. (Mrs. Fine nudged elbows with Richard. Sara knew she was caught in a fib but was going to try to get out of it).

Sara: Sara told Mrs. Fine she was exhausted from travelling all day. I would like to get my picture now if I can?

I also wanted you to autograph this photo I took of you and Mr. Fine from Baltimore.

Leena: Sure Sara. Come over here. Is your flash on your Camera?

Sara: I think it's okay without the flash.

Leena: Okay. Come stand by me Sara.

Sara: (walks over to Mrs. Fine) Mrs. Fine's worker grabs Sara camera and takes a picture). Thank you, Mrs. Fine. I'm sorry I didn't catch you I the hall. I was really tired and I didn't want to get on line twice and wait for Mr. Fine. It would be too long for me.

Mrs. Fine: You took a great picture of us at the convention. Thank you for stopping by and it was nice seeing you.

Sara: I will see you tomorrow in the Photo Op room.

My cousin is coming in and we are taking picture with you and Mr. Fine.

Sara: (Was feeling kind of guilty when taking the photo). Thank you again.

Mrs. Fine: Your welcome Sara. Are you okay Sara?

Sara: I'm okay Mrs. Fine. Thank you.

Leena: Richard!

Richard: Wait a minute!

Darling I'm signing autographs. What is it?

Leena: (Nudged Richard and elbowed him).

Richard: What is it darling.

Leena: Sara looks upset. I think she lied again about that guy.

Richard: (Finished signing autographs and looked up at Leena) I will question her tomorrow in the photo op. I won't tell her when I see her on line?

Leena: I'd like to see her reaction. I know she knows something.

Richard: She's just scared.

Sara walked over to Marie St. John. And she introduced herself to Mrs. St. John.

Sara: Hello Mrs. St. John, my name is Sara.

Marie St. John: Hello Sara it's nice to meet you. How are you?

Sara: I am fine. I am a big fan of Bonding is a Crime and Riker's Hospital. I think you're an actress and wonderful writer/producer.

Marie St. John: Thank you Sara. Thank you so much. I'm so very tired. I just flew in today from Los Angeles, California.

Sara: I know what you mean I came in from Poughkeepsie, New York. Not a bad ride, but I took the longer route because I enjoy travelling and the scenery this time of year.

Marie St. John: What can I do for you Sara?

Sara: I'd like a picture with you.

Marie St. John: That would be great Sara. Let's do one. Marie asked her worker to grab Sara's camera and take a picture.

Sara: (Sara sat next to Marie).

Marie: It was so nice of you to come to all the signings for Riker's Hospital.

Sara: Thank you Mrs. St. John. It was nice meeting you.

Marie: You too Sara.

Sara got up and walked out of the room. She recognized some of the fans from the club and said hello to them. She waived to them and then she went to see the rest of the cast from Riker's Hospital.

Chapter 17

The Omen's Call 666

Back in room 666, Roy was really pissed off he couldn't get to Mr. Fine.

He took out Mr. and Mrs. Fine's photo from Baltimore. Then a red pen.

Roy: (holds up Mr. Fine's photo) Damn you Mr. Fine **DAMN! DAMN! DAMN!** First, he crinkled the photo then he said wait a minute I has a better idea. You do look familiar to me so I'm going to save this photo.

He took Mr. Fine's photo and drew it up with a sad face. **Sad! Sad! Sad!** He exclaimed! Then he took his serrated pocket knife and sliced it. You might have got one on me tonight Mr. Fine. But I will fix you tomorrow. I should have taken care of all of you in Maryland. I will definitely fix you tomorrow Mr. Fine!

I will be your worst nightmare! You know the nightmares you had when you were a kid??? Huh?? Well It's Nothing Compared to What You're going to have tomorrow night! NOTHING! NOTHING! (his rage was getting louder and louder).

Roy took out the other photo of Mr. Fine and decided to make copies. It was still early enough and the computer room on the other side of the hotel was opened. Roy put everything in a folder and then he went to the front desk at the other hotel. He figured Mr. and Mrs. Fine were on the lobby floor of the hotel room. That's where all the large suites were.

Roy figured to make about five hundred copies. Man, that's expensive he thought. But he said to himself it's well worth it when it comes to Richard Fine.

Roy: (talking to himself) You're definitely a fraud but who are you really? I honestly just don't have time to follow it up right now but I will in the future. When Roy was finished, he went back to his to figure out how to fold them or put them in Mr. Fine's room.

Roy: God. I'm not sure what to do? Do I fold it horizontally or vertically? Or, should I slip it under the door. Hymm.. Tricky. This guy is so damn annoying. I'm really tired and I have to figure out when and how I'm going to torment Fine.

I wished they had a website for answers on this. Roy decided to fold them vertically and stick them in by the door knob.

Meanwhile, Sara was roaming around downstairs and exploring the different vender stores. She decided to take photos with more celebrities from Riker's Hospital. She went fast and met five cast members from Riker's Hospital because it started getting really late. The actors were packing it in. Sara was so excited when she saw the actor Doctor Rick from Riker's Hospital and the lab technician walking by, that she took quick pictures. She thought she saw some other characters from the show but she figured she was over tired. It was getting late and Sara went to bed.

The hotel venders shut down and celebrities closed their tables for the evening. They covered their tables and went back to their room. Roy came down from his room with all the pictures of Mr. Fine neatly folded. They were stacked neatly in his manila folder. Roy went to every door and put a picture of Mr. Fine on it. He decided to put A non-threatening picture of Mr. Fine on it so people would not get suspicious. It took him about an hour to cover all the doors when he got done handing out all the flyers, he decided to go back to his room and go to sleep.

The next morning was Saturday. Sara woke up but she decided to sleep in late until at least nine o clock. She knew Jean was coming and that she wanted to be ready and downstairs. Jean texted Sara at around nine o clock and said she'd be there like eleven or eleven thirty in the lobby. Sara stretched out a bit and did her morning stretch routine.

Then she took a shower and did her hair. She decided to go downstairs and go to the buffet for breakfast. Sara went to the restaurant buffet for breakfast. They had delicious breakfast items to choose from: pancakes, bacon, potatoes, hash browns, eggs, sausage, toast, eggs benedict on one side with Danishes, and muffins. Another counter had different beverages like, teas, and juices. The third counter had different breads. There was toast, bagels, English muffins and different jellies, syrups, butters, and cream cheese all displayed so neatly in heart shapes. It looked so yummy. Sara wanted everything and eat everything. But she lost so much weight that she knew she had to control herself.

Sara grabbed breakfast and sat at one of the tables. She had coffee and toast. She saw some fans and said hello. After breakfast Sara went for a walk and saw more actors from Riker's Hospital. She saw Doctor John who the show use to call John Boy because he's been on the show since he was a kid and Nurse Holliman. It was getting close to 11:30 and Jean texted Sara to say she was arriving in the front and in the parking lot of Graveyard Theater. Sara texted her back and said she would meet her at the front entrance of the lobby. Jean finally parked her car and met up with Sara in the lobby. Sara asked the concierge attendant to take Jean's luggage up to her room. The concierge attendant grabbed all Jean's luggage and put it on a rolling cart and took it upstairs. Sara and Jean walked around. They had about an hour to spare because they were doing photo ops with the Fines.

Sara: You're going to see Mr. Fine again and meet Mrs. Fine.

Jean: Is she nice?

Sara: She's very nice and gorgeous! She's so pretty. We have a photo op with them and the cast from Rikers's Hospital.

Jean: Cool I love that show.

Sara: Yeah and Doctor John is over there.

Jean: He's seriously cute.

Sara: I think we should get our pictures with him and Nurse Mia there too.

Jean: Cool.

Sara: Look (Sara points) over there is the Chief of Staff, Nurse Mia and Dr. Rick.

Jean: Wow. How exciting I can't wait to get my picture with them. I want my

picture with Doctor John first. I want to ask him if he's going to marry nurse Mia.

Sara: You're brave. I want to ask him that. I will let you manipulate him.

Jean: Hah! Hah! Hah! (laughs) you are sneaky.

Sara: I'm not sneaky I'm slippery. Why don't you tell him he's a great actor and him and Mia have good chemistry? Hee heel... (laughs)

Jean: Yeah, I like that idea. Okay come on.

Sara and Jean walk up to where Doctor John is signing autographs from Riker's Hospital.

There were no fans there. Sara first walked up and introduced herself.

Sara: Hi I'm Sara. I love Rikers's Hospital and your role as Doctor John.

Doctor John: Thank you thank you so much.

Jean: You and Mia have such great chemistry. You are so good together. Any plans on the characters getting married.

Doctor John: So far no. We just got our new scripts. But we start dating again.

Jean: Hope there's a big wedding.

Doctor John: Would you like a picture with me?

Sara and Jean: Both say Yes.

Sara: See I behaved myself.

Doctor John: Laughed.

Jean: Laughed. Sara, Jean and Doctor John all posed for a picture. Then Sara wanted a separate picture with the doctor.

After that, they walked over to Nurse Mia and took their picture with her. Sara and Jean both introduced themselves to Nurse Mia. They both got their picture taken with her. It was getting close to taking pictures with the cast from Riker's Hospital and Mr. and Mrs. Fine. Sara kept getting the times mixed up with who they were taken pictures with. Sara and Jean started heading to the elevator doors. Sara pressed the up button for the second floor.

Sara: Do you want to take a picture with the Fines?

Jean: No.

Sara: Oh, come on Sara don't make me go in there alone with Mr. and Mrs. Fine.

Jean: I really just want the cast from Riker's Hospital.

The elevator doors open to take them to the second floor. Sara and Jean got in. They went up to the photo op room. They walked down one corridor and then turn right down another corridor. Then they turned left twice down another corridor. Sara stopped because she heard two guests complaining to the hotel maids.

Guests: We just got these photos in our door. Do you know who put them there. There in all the doors.

Sara: (looked at Jean). Look at that. That's really weird and it's of Mr. Fine. That guy is in this hotel that was harassing him was at the Revue. I'm wondering if he's up to something?

Jean: Really. that stinks for Mr. Fine

Sara: Yes, security is watching him. I'm scared. But let's go. We have two more hallways to go down.

Sara and Jean continue to walk to the photo op room. The lines were crazy. Many of the same fans were on line. Security again asked people to wait up against the wall because celebrities needed to walk by.

Security: No photos of celebs. All cameras need to be put away.

Jean: (Turns to Sara). Don't even think about it.

Sara: (Laughed). We should send one to Robert.

Jean: (Laughed). NO!

The lines were moving slowly. It took about an hour in a half to get into the photo op room.

Sara and Jean got online. They went in one room and got them picture taken with the cast of Riker's Hospital. Then they went outside to wait online in a different room to see Mr. and Mrs. Fine. Jean was animate about not going. Sara and Jean knew they had to wait at least over an hour for the Fines.

Sara: Are you sure you don't want to come in with me Jean. Come on please? I don't want to go in there with Mr. and Mrs. Fine all by myself (Sara knew Mr. Fine was going to ask questions and she tried to manipulate Jean to come in so she wouldn't have to answer them). Come on Jean I will pay you an extra hundred if you come in? I'm afraid the Fines will question me.

Soon after Sara said that the Fines walked in and walked down the hall into the other Photo Op. Mrs. Fine walked first and went up to Sara to say hello. Mr. Fine walked around Mrs. Fine and completely ignored Sara.

Sara: (turns to Jean) Man they always catch me. See Mr. Fine? He knows I'm not telling the truth. They must know I'm not telling the whole truth.

Jean: Well, shouldn't you tell them the truth?

Sara: I want to but there's never the right time to tell the truth or enough time. I guess I'm going in by myself. Plus, they are celebrities. They won't listen to some peon like me.

Jean: Yes, you are going by yourself. I'm not bailing you out of this one.

Mrs. Fine: (walks in the room and elbows Richard) Did you hear Sara asking the other girl to come in and get the picture?

Mr. Fine: No. You must have bionic ears. Leena. I will question her when she gets here. It's too bad I couldn't get her in the back alone. She's going to be with her cousin. But if not, I will question her. I will play a game of devil's advocate with her.

While Sara and Jean were talking, Roy was back in Room 666 and he was at his desk. He was practicing making a phone call to the front desk saying there was a bomb. He was feeling back to normal after being so upset.

Roy: Hi. You have a bomb in your building. Na that's not good enough. How about. A whispery voice. There's a bomb in the hotel. Do you know where?? Or in an evil low tone voice. There's a bomb in the building. Or Maybe… Hey how ya doing you know there's a bomb in the building. This is Richard Fine. Ooh! Yes..

Picks his lip. .. I really like that one. I made a joke, makes them look stupid and then makes me laugh. Wait a minute! I have it (in an English accent). Oh! There's a bomb in your building. This is Richard Fine coming live.

Then I can disguise my voice. Hymm… (Roy scratches his cheek. Then he picks his nose and nails. Then he rubs his hands together.) Yes. that's the way to do it. I have to do some warm up exercises, then I will call. It was getting late about 3:30 pm. Roy picks up the phone and puts it down. Sara and Jean are up next for the photo op.

Meanwhile back on the Photo Op line Jean and Sara are chatting and getting ready to take photos with Mr. Fine. Sara is begging Jean to come in.

Jean: I will wait out here for you.

Sara: Please Jean come in.

Jean: You are on your own. Tell Mr. Fine. what you know. He won't be mad with you.

Sara: Well yeah. That's true. There can't be consequences. But he's a powerful man.

Jean: Go tell him the truth.

Sara: Oh, All Right.

It was Sara's turn to go in the photo op room. Sara walked in to see Mr. and Mrs. Fine.

Mr. Fine: I need to ask you something Sara as he held her back ever so gently. and put Sara's ear against his lips. Sara wasn't thrilled and was becoming tense.

Mrs. Fine: (grabbed Sara's arm) What is it Sara?

Sara: (Sara didn't know what to say.) Sara opened up to Mr. Fine. I heard some stuff.

Mr. Fine: What kind of stuff??

Photographer: Time to take a picture. The photographer took their photo.

Sara: You got some interesting people in this building I mean. (Sara *was about to come clean with Mr. Fine)*

Then the fire alarm went off over 1,000 people on the second floor had to evacuate the photo op room. Jean got Sara. They went slowly downstairs with hundreds of people while the celebrities, guests staff evacuated the Graveyard Theater Hotel. Sara was taking pictures of everyone leaving and existing out of the building.

The fire alarm was so loud it continued on for several minutes. Jean and Sara stood out in the cold rainstorm. It was very windy standing out in the middle of a Nor Easter Storm. They didn't have any jackets or umbrellas.

Police and other emergency response teams showed up at the scene.

Staff were escorting guest outside the hotel telling everyone there was a gas leak. Many guests stayed in the entrance walkway outside the hotel because they didn't have an umbrella and wanted to stay out of the rain. Others were in the street watching police offers directed people where to go. Some guests left and decided to do other things. Reporters were at the scene taking photos.

No one was allowed at the side of the building except for security. However, Sara and Jean decided to go to their car and get warm. A very handsome officer came up to Jeans window and told Jean they couldn't stay there it was too dangerous. Jean and Sara got out of the car and waited a bit longer out in the cold, windy storm, to see what was happening. After about an hour standing in the cold rainy storm a police officer came up to the crowd and said "PLEASE STEP ONE HUNDRED FEET BACK."

Sara: (Turns to Jean) I think it's time we left. I don't like this.

Jean: Yes. I see cars leaving too. Somethings wrong.

Sara and Jean walk to Jean's car. They get in and pull away from the building. The rain is pouring. People are standing outside with a coat on and blankets over their heads. Many were without umbrellas and had to stand underneath where there was a roof. Sara and Jean took off. Jean pulled around by the circular entrance of the hotel. She pulled up to a handsome Police officer.

Police Officer: It's going to be awhile Ma'am. A few more hours. Someone called in a bomb threat!

Jean: Okay. Thank you. (turns to Sara) We are getting out of here.

Sara: (Sara didn't make the connection about Roy and was too shaken up) Wow. Holy Toledo! That's Scary.

Jean: Yeah. I know. Where do you want to go?

Sara: How about the Marriotti. Or another hotel.

Jean: Let's do the Marriotti. Oh my god it's freaking cold.

Sara: I'm going to try to warn Mr. and Mrs. Fine I want to contact their webmaster who runs the Facebook club to tell them their fans to be careful.

Jean: Good idea.

Jean and Sara arrived at the Marriotti and went to the restaurant bar and grill. Many of the fans ended up there. Jean and Sara were invited to have drinks. Many were tipsy as it was.

Sara: Sara was still so scared and shocked at everything for she wasn't thinking and wondering if Roy had anything to do with it. She got so preoccupied and asked for a Jagermeister. She got so preoccupied and asked for Jagermeister by accident. Two fans at the end of the bar either laughed at Sara or were just laughing among themselves. Their timing was a bit off and it looked a bit rude. Sara honestly wanted to laugh with them. But Sara had too much on her mind and apologized to the bartender.

Bartender: Did you mean Jägermeister?

Sara: Yes. Sorry about that. Just so much on the mind.

Bartender: That's okay.

Jean: I will have a bear.

Sara: Now it's really time to drink.

Jean: Laughs.

Sara: (turns to Jean as she takes a sip). Do you think it could be that guy?

Jean: It's not an impossibility. I mean anything is possible.

Sara: Mr. Fine was asking me questions in the photo op.

Jean: About that guy who was arrogant in NY?

Sara: Yes. He followed Mr. Fine to Baltimore and then here in New Jersey.

Jean: Yeah That's creepy. I hope they investigate him more.

Sara: I know what you mean. I will call the police department tomorrow and report him again.

Then this morning I received a photo of Mr. Fine. I forgot to ask him if he put it on my door to advertise for his book signing.

Jean: Well why would he want to walk up and down the hallways. He couldn't have possible done it. He is signing autographs all afternoon.

Sara: (thought about it). Yeah, you're right. He was in the autograph room. It's just so creepy. I'm wondering if that guy did something? You want to order a set of nachos and some appetizers.

Jean: Yes. That will hold us over. Let's see what's on the news first. Maybe we can start heading back to the hotel.

Sara: Excuse me Bartender. We like an order of Nachos and potato skins in a few minutes. We just need a few minutes to watch the news.

Bartender: Would you like another drink?

Sara: Yes.

Sara and Jean sat at the bar for about another hour eating and drinking. One of the fans said look up on the screen. Sara and Jean looked up and saw themselves on the news stepping one hundred feet back.

Sara: Wow! They said it's almost time to go back inside. That the gas leak was fixed and waiting on news on the bomb scare.

Jean: I bet you it's okay. We could start heading back, I think!

One of the fans got a text and said the hotel was clear. Sara and Jean paid their bill and thanked the bartender for his service. They gave him a nice tip and left the hotel. When they got back it was dark outside and still rain. FBI, three or four police departments, paramedics, first responders were still outside. Many guests started waiting by the entrance doors of the hotel. The rain finally stopped. Sara and Jean waited with the other guests in the front entrance of the hotel. Then police officer came out and told everyone it was okay to go back inside. All the guests headed back inside.

Chapter 18

False Alarm

Everyone went back into the hotel. Sara went to visit Mr. and Mrs. Fine. She waited online for several minutes. Many celebrities were not at their desks. The security guards asked fans to give celebrities about a half hour or more to collect their thoughts and get organized. Sara and Jean waited. They had reservations to go to the Steakhouse. The security guard came out of the autograph room and told fans that Mr. and Mrs. Fine had to leave for New York City. They may come back tomorrow. Sara and Jean overheard fans talking. One fan saw Mr. and Mrs. Fine leave with the FBI

Sara: (looks to Jean) Wow! Somethings up!

Jean: Yes. Definitely but what?

Sara: I don't know. . . you want to go to the Steakhouse? Then have some fun and do room service for dessert? I think I'm going early tomorrow. I'm exhausted. I hope I run into Mr. and Mrs. Fine. I will contact their webmaster.

Jean: Yes! Let's celebrate our birthdays and have some fun with it.

Jean and Sara went to the Steakhouse to celebrate their birthdays. They went back to their rooms and ordered dessert and watched television.

They decided to leave early the next morning. Jean took Sara to the bus station.

Sara had many questions on her mind with Mr. and Mrs. Fine.

Roy went back to his studio apartment in Los Angeles, California where he's been living for the last twenty years. Roy was a bit disappointed that he couldn't carry out everything he had hoped for with the Fines. But he knew for some reason he recognized the Fines.

Roy unpacked all his pictures. He put his things away and put his pictures on the mahogany table. He took out Mr. and Mrs. Fine's photo and stared at them for a while.

Roy: God. These two looks really really familiar. Especially Mrs. Fine. But where did I see her?

Roy was a big soap opera fan of Riker's Hospital but couldn't recognizes Leena's photo. He thought about it for a while.

Roy: Well they would have to be a wealthy couple if they were undercover and have money to do this type of stuff. But who could they be? They hung around the cast of Riker's Hospital but didn't talk much to the Riker's Hospital's cast but yet they all knew each other. Was one of them on Riker's Hospital? I mean Mrs. Fine is gorgeous enough to play a role. I'm wondering if she played a role? I know she wrote for the show.

Roy logs into his computer system and goes to the cast of Riker's Hospital. He sees the whole cast and doesn't see the Fines. Then Roy thought that maybe she was on the show awhile back. He researches it from the 1970s but still no Mr. or Mrs. Fine. Roy researches Riker's Hospital in the 80's and sees a photo similar to Mrs. Fines.

What does Roy Think?

Chapter 19

Ransom Note

It's been a few days since the bomb scare. One morning the Fines woke up in their home. The doorbell rang.

Leena: I will get it Darling. Whisky follows Leena downstairs the front door. Leena opens the door and it's the UPS man. The UPS man delivers a bubble letter to Leena and Leena signs off UPS, thank you. Have a great day. Mrs. Fine walks into the kitchen and open up the bubble envelope and she pull out a typed letter.

Dear Mr. and Mrs. Fine:

If you want to see your daughter alive again it will cost you 100,000. Call police and she will die. You have five days to get the money. I will be sending you another letter through UPS in five days to tell you when and where to drop off the money.

Your daughter Lynn is with me and still alive. If you want to see your daughter again, I would suggest you come up with the ransom and I want the money in $100. Bills. No police, No FBI, No law enforcement or Lynn dies.

I will be watching your house to make sure you are not contacting anyone. I will send you a letter or call your number. "By the way, Your Daughter Is A Pretty Bitch." Ha Ha Ha.

Great speeches at your book signing events. Especially at Graveyard.

Mrs. Fine: (Screams) Richard! Richard! Hurry and come quick! Richard!

Mr. Fine: What is it Leena?

Leena: (Hands Mr. Fine the ransom Letter). Look Richard it's a ransom Letter. It looks like Lynn was kidnapped. She's Alive!

Mr. Fine: That could be a fake letter Leena. It's been over two weeks. If she was kidnapped, we would have received a ransom letter much earlier or at least I would have thought. Why would kidnappers wait two in a half week for $100,000? Whisky came into the kitchen wagging his tale and Leena picked him up and put him on her lap. She started petting him. I will call detective Dunim.

Richard picks up the phone and calls Laura.

Mr. Fine: Hello Laura, it's Richard Fine on the line. How are you?

Laura: Good Mr. Fine How are you?

Mr. Fine: I was just calling to see if there was any news on Lynn.

Laura: No News. Why is something wrong?

Mr. Fine: Yes. The UPS man stopped by our house this morning and dropped off an envelope.

My wife opened up the envelope and It was a ransom note from kidnappers, saying they have Lynn and want $100,000. What do I do? They don't want police involved, FBI or law enforcement and says we won't see Lynn again.

Laura: Okay, I will be over with Detective Briggs in about sixty minutes. I want to examine the note. What time did UPS come?

Mr. Fine: About 11:15 A.M.

Laura: Maybe I can figure out what UPS office it came from and narrow the UPS stores down. Have that information with the mail and receipt ready for me when I come. We will be there in about sixty minutes. Turn on the news. Briggs is doing a press conference on the slayings and kidnappings near Hotel Chiller.

Mr. Fine: Okay Laura thank you. I appreciate it.

Mrs. Fine: Darling, I am scared for Lynn. What if this is fake?? If it's real, we could be putting her in danger.

Mr. Fine: Well the thing is is that Laura came on my book signing events and people know who she is so I think it will be okay to include her. They think she's a worker in my hotel. We will only ask her and Detective Briggs to help us out.

Mr. Fine grabs both of Mrs. Fine's arms and rubs them down. We will be okay. This will work trust me. In the meantime, lets watch some television and turn on the news. Laura said that there is a press conference about the kidnappings.

Mr. Fine was in the kitchen. After he hung up the phone, he grabbed the two dogs' dishes. One he filled with water and one with food. Whisky started eating. Mr. Fine didn't put down Scotch's plate and kept it on the counter. They never know where Scotch is. Then put it down. Whisky started eating. He got the remote to his television and turned it on.

Mrs. Fine: Darling turn the television set up: Look there's a news story our hotel is on television.

News Caster: (starring into the camera, and then pointing down at the lake)

"The third body this morning was found faced down near Lake Ravine here, not too far from Hotel Chiller in Los Angeles. Police don't know much yet of who the remains of this person are. They know it's a young female with reddish medium hair. She was faced down here near the creek. (as he walks over) Police have cut off this area for further investigation. There were two missing persons two weeks ago. One was Marie Rays another was Lynn Fine. We are just waiting on dental records to confirm that this is Marie Rays. Since Marie disappeared first, we believe the body is hers. Police are thinking this was her remains that were found.

This is the third victim in four months. Now we are going to hear from Detective Briggs of the Los Angeles County Sheriff's Department. Back to you.

The detective is holding a press conference at the Los Angeles Police Department and there are several reporters and cameras listening to him speaking. The detective comes out and stands before the podium. Detective AJ Briggs is tall with blond hair and brown eyes. He was wearing a gray jacket black shirt and pants.

Detective Briggs:

Good Morning! My name is Detective Anthony Briggs. I am investigating the murders that are happening near Lake Ravine in Los Angeles. So far, we have three victims. Our third victim was found face down. She looks like she was strangled and she was found with a bag over her face. Her hands were also tied in surgical tape and pieces of surgical tape was found near her wrists. We think she is Marie Rays from Los Angeles. We are waiting on dental records now to confirm this.

She is definitely a part of the investigation of the Lake Ravine murders in Los Angeles. She was last seen leaving Hotel Chiller in Los Angeles and her vehicle was found at Brentwood Mall.

This is definitely connected to the Lake Ravine stalking and slayings.

The first victim Susan Stone age twenty-two of Los Angeles. The second victim Denise Morris from Los Angeles age twenty-five. All three victims have red hair, and have been found near Lake Ravine two weeks after their disappearance. FBI think these victims are held in captivity for a while for about a week until they are murdered. They all have been last seen leaving Hotel Chiller in Los Angeles and disappeared near Brentwood Mall. In addition, these victims all have been strangled and found with a bag on their face.

They are all between the ages of twenty-three and twenty-five. We are asking the public for information and seeking help from the community. Anyone with information on these murders are asked to help and greatly appreciated. We feel we are getting closer to the killer and narrowing down where and who is he is. We also believe these girls have been abducted in broad daylight at Brentwood Mall. I believe our kidnapper and killer makes it simple to throw off law enforcement. I am going to hold up three photos of these victims and show the public.

Detective Briggs holds up the first photo of victim number one: This is Susan Stone. Susan was last seen at Hotel Chiller. Her car was found at Brentwood Mall. She could have been at Brentwood Mall shopping. Next photo is of Denise Morris. Denise was also at Hotel Chiller and then her vehicle was found at Brentwood Mall. Our third victim is Marie Rays. Lynn Fine went missing almost two weeks ago.

Marie was a worker at Hotel Chiller and she went to Brentwood Mall. Her car disappeared. If anyone has seen these workers near Brentwood Mall please call the Chiller Hotline or Los Angeles Police Department. I will be taking questions from reporters.

Also, too a tipster called in that there is a suspicious person hanging around Brentwood Mall approaching girls during the day and showing them perfume samples. If you see anyone doing this do not approach him. The perfume could be laced with drugs. This is how he may be getting his victims in the car. He probably keeps them in captivity until the drug wears off.

Reporter #1: Is there any connection to Lynn Fine's kidnappings?

Briggs: That hasn't been confirmed. We haven't found her body.

Reporter #2: Is there a chance Lynn Fine could still be alive?

Briggs: Yes, there is.

Reporter #3: Has anyone come forward with information on any of these murders?

Briggs: We have received a few phone calls but no real leads. The only suspicious one was the person selling perfume samples and having people smell them. We have one lead right now, which I will be following up on. We aren't yet allowed to disclose information on what we found. I can tell you there is evidence that Lynn Fine is still alive. We do know that the killer does keep his victim in captivity for about two weeks before he kills them. It's only been a week in a half since Lynn Fine's disappearance.

We will be holding another brief conference in a few days to confirm the body that was found by Lake Ravine and update on Lynn's disappearance. I want to hold up a picture of Lynn Fine.

This is Lynn Fine. She has medium length reddish hair. She is about 5 foot 4 inches tall with gray eyes, last seen leaving Hotel Chiller and her car was at Brentwood Mall. I'm putting her picture up now while there is a chance, she's alive and we can get some leads to lead to where she could be being held captive.

About two hours passed by and the doorbell rang. Anyone seen any strange incidences occur at Hotel Chiller or Brentwood please contact the Los Angeles Police Department. Finally, anyone knows of any strange houses deserted or condemned looking suspicious please call.

Reporter #4: I know this may sound stupid.

Briggs: Go ahead we are listening for any help.

Reporter #4: Could this be related to any of the bomb threats that occurred at

Graveyard Theater in New Jersey the other day? Rumors had it that the Lynn's mother and father were at the book signing event and they had to leave early. Could there be any connection to who called in the bomb threat and Lynn's disappearance in New Jersey??

Briggs: That question was never brought up but I will look into it and discuss this with my fellow colleagues and put in some calls to see if they have a suspect's name and address. Thanks for the question. We will be back here in a few days with an update. Again, any leads, suspicious activity, surrounding these events or even if you were in Graveyard Theater in New Jersey with events, and know of suspicious activity please call. There is nothing wrong in reporting something suspicious. All calls will be kept confidential and I will personally thank each tipster. Please if you see anyone suspicious hanging around Brentwood Mall approaching people call police immediately. Don't hesitate! Do Not Approach Anyone selling samples of perfume. Please report it to police or call 911, even if it's a fake, it needs to be investigated. No stone will go uncovered.

You can also ask for Detective Briggs as well. Help from the community is greatly appreciated. We will be airing another segment on Lynn Fine tomorrow evening on this station from the panel discussion with the Fines at the Convention Center from Maryland. "It will be called In Pursuit to Stop A Killing."

Mr. Fine: Leena did you hear Briggs??

Lenna: Wiping her eyes from crying. Yes, I did. I just can't help but feel we are missing something. Mr. and Mrs. Fine was watching Briggs speak out on his daughter.

Mr. Fine: Maybe our answers will come when Laura and Briggs get here. Laura texted me and said she would be a little bit. So maybe they are getting calls and tips in right now as we speak.

Let Me read that letter again. Leena hands Richard the letter. Richard reviews the letter and reads it one more time quietly. The both sat together for about an hour before Laura and detective Briggs arrived.

Laura: Rang the doorbell.

Mrs. Fine: I will get it darling. Whisky follows Mrs. Fine to the door wagging his tail barking. Whisky sits by Mrs. Fine's feet wagging his tale and Mrs. Fine answers the door. Who is it?

Laura: Detective Briggs from the Los Angeles Police Department.

Mrs. Fine opens the door and she kiss Laura. Laura introduces Mrs. Fine to Detective Briggs.

Whisky is barking very very loud, and jumps on Laura wagging his tail. Laura pets him and scratches underneath his neck. Whisky is licking and playing with Laura.

Mrs. Fine: Whisky get down.

Laura: It's okay he's fine.

Whisky jumps on Briggs and starts playing with Briggs. They all walk into the kitchen and Mr. Fine shakes Laura's hand. He gives her a big kiss. Laura introduces Detective Briggs to Mr. Fine.

Mr. Fine: I have the note the kidnappers sent us. I am reading it and something in the last sentence doesn't make sense. Laura do you want to read it?

Laura: Yes. Let me have a look.

They all sit around the kitchen table. Mrs. Fine has tea, coffee, water, and juice out. She also took out Danishes and bagels.

Mrs. Fine: (wiping her tears) I am still so very upset and worried.

Laura: We believe your daughter is alive Mrs. Fine. I want to review this letter and read it out loud. We need to put our minds together and brainstorm clues. I need everyone to be emotionally calm and maintain composure. Maybe we can figure out how to rescue Lynn and find Lynn before the third week approaches. That's when he goes off. Mrs. Fine do you have paper and pens??

Mrs. Fine: Yes, I do. I have two legal pads.

Laura: Okay. What I want to do is for you to get me the paper and pens. Then we should get into groups of two. Detective Briggs you sit with Mrs. Fine, and I will sit with Mr. Fine, since I spent much time with him. Briggs you take Mrs. Fine a go inside the living room and Mr. Fine and I will work in the kitchen.

Jot down your thoughts after I read this letter and discuss it quietly in the living room. We will discuss it for forty-five minutes and come back to this table and meet. Okay?

All of them say got it!

Briggs: Okay. Mrs. Fine why don't you grab a chair by me.

Laura: Mr. Fine come sit by me.

Whisky went by Mrs. Fine again and sat by her legs.

Laura: I'm going to read this letter out loud to all and then we are going to break

apart write down strange things from this letter.

Laura: Reads the ransom Note:

Dear Mr. and Mrs. Fine:

If you want to see your daughter alive again it will cost you 100,000. Call police and it she will die. I will call you first and ask you . . . Ha Ha.

You have five days to get the money. I will be sending you another letter through UPS in five days to tell you when and where to drop off the money.

Your daughter Lynn is with me and still alive. If you want to see your daughter again, I would suggest you come up with the ransom and I want the money in $100. Bills. No police, No FBI, No law enforcement or Lynn dies.

I will be watching your house to make sure you are not contacting anyone. I will send you a letter or call your number. "By the way, Your Daughter Is A Pretty Bitch." Ha Ha Ha

Great speeches at your book signing events. Especially at Graveyard.

Laura: Okay, so we are all clear on what the letter said. I will read this one more time and really think about it. I will write down an extra letter for my records. Laura reads and writes the letter down.

Dear Mr. and Mrs. Fine:

If you want to see your daughter alive again it will cost you 100,000. Call police and it she will die. You have five days to get the money. I will be sending you another letter through UPS in five days to tell you when and where to drop off the money.

Your daughter Lynn is with me and still alive. If you want to see your daughter again, I would suggest you come up with the ransom and I want the money in $100. Bills. No police, No FBI, No law enforcement or Lynn dies.

I will be watching your house to make sure you are not contacting anyone. I will send you a letter or call your number. "By the way, Your Daughter Is A Pretty Bitch." Ha Ha Ha

Great speeches at your book signing events. Especially at Graveyard.

When Laura was finished, she handed her copy to Detective Briggs and Mrs. Fine. Mrs. Fine, Detective Briggs and Whisky went into the living room.

Mr. Fine: Sits with Laura.

Mr. Fine: See how in the middle he says I but it could mean more than one too.

Laura: Yes. It's every other word is I. He's not the smartest criminal. See where it says pretty bitch. And great speeches at your book signing events at Graveyard?

Mr. Fine: Yes. He must have been at some of the signings. If he was then maybe there are two involved.

Laura: He had to be at least two involved I would say. If he was at the book signing events then someone else had Lynn. Okay. So, who was upsetting you at the book signing event? Oh! Wait a minute. Pretty Bitch! "That's what that guy said in the bathroom to me in NYC!" He must have been in NYC at your book signing event with Lisa Smith.

Mr. Fine: I heard that at my book signing event in Madison too. So, he was at the events. Then there was Graveyard Theater where security had to stop this guy because he was going around harassing my fans. He was removed from my line. Even before our dinner party with the fans, I had to pull him off of Leena. Then there was the bomb threat at Graveyard that Saturday. I wonder if it's the same person. He had a creepy looking eye.

Laura: Interesting.

Meanwhile forty minutes past and Mrs. Fine and Detective Briggs came back into the kitchen and Whisky followed them in and sat by Mrs. Fine's feet licking her shoes and biting off laces.

Leena: Stop Whisky,..as she pets him. Okay Richard. So, this is what I came up with. The week you were at the book signing event with Lisa Smith in NYC, I received a weird call. I told you about this the night you came home. It was about 9pm and the caller said Pretty Bitch.

Laura: Stop right there.

Mrs. Fine: What Is It.

Laura: I was almost attacked in the bathroom that same night at 9pm and when I was in the bathroom my attacker made a phone call and said pretty bitch. Come to think about it, when I peeked to get a look, he looked like he had a phone in his hand, but I couldn't tell. He was probably calling you. He had a weird looking eye too.

Mrs. Fine: Did you call police?

Laura: I called security and filled out a report. We need to get cameras from NYC book signing event. Maybe one of the fans took pictures.

Mr. Fine: Well Mrs. Fine and I were concerned about one fan Sara. She was afraid of someone following me and reported it to security. She maybe in my Facebook group I can contact me webmaster to find out.

Laura: Yes. We want to talk to her. She may have information for us.

Mrs. Fine: Also, there was that guy at the bar that my husband had to throw out who was harassing me and that guy who was harassing Richard's fans too. He had a weird looking eye and white hair.

Laura: Yes, we have that down. Is it the same guy??

Mr. Fine: Yes. It's the same guy who Sara saw too.

Laura: Okay. We need to speak to Sara.

Mr. Fine: I know her name is Sara Novella and She was with another person, Jean Novella and Robert Novella.

Laura: I can track them down just by you giving me their name. Maybe they have stuff on camera and help us out. What else do we have?? I will call the hotel to get a list of guests who stayed.

Obviously, he stayed there so there has to be a name. Maybe we can narrow it down by a picture and time as well.

Mrs. Fine: Well I received a flyer in the hotel room with our picture on it. I didn't tell anyone because I thought it was a fan. Maybe you can ask the hotel if anyone else had flyers on us.

Laura: I will definitely ask. I think we got everything for now. I don't think we need any more information at the moment. We got Sara Novella. She's are biggest shot. The cameras at Graveyard may help. Hopefully she is smart enough and will call our department with information. I don't think we need any more information. I think that could be our guy.

Someone may have a personal issue with Mr. Fine. He kidnapped and killed three girls who were at your hotel at one point and then followed you to Graveyard Hotel.

Mr. Fine: Wait. The night we came back from NYC, we thought someone was on the property. I have cameras and could look back. I think it would be dark though.

Laura: Nc. But if it could catch a car or license plate number it helps us track things down.

Mr. Fine: Okay. I am going to review my camera for that night in a little bit. If I can't see the person, I will look for an automobile. It was out towards the back so I know what and where to look at.

Laura*:* I wouldn't worry too much about him watching your house. If he does, we just pull up the camera now one more time. So, it's a good thing you told me. I just think it's only two people and he cannot be watching your house, working and kidnapping all at once. He would need more manpower. Asking for $100,000 sounds to me like one or two people and someone who know you. Do you know who would have a jealousy issue with you??

Mr. Fine: The only one who does come to mind is Roy Martin from Riker's Hospital.

Laura: Oh yes. The one who murdered three people from the show back in the eighties right??

Mr. Fine: Right! They wanted my daughter to play the part of his daughter and bring her on to the show at the time, but I wouldn't allow it. He attacked my wife on the set. He went to jail but was released about a year ago.

Laura: Interesting. He was Roy Martin Right?

Mr. Fine: Yes.

Laura: Okay. I'm going to research him too and question him. Maybe something there.

Chapter 20

Roy's Karma

A few days passed by and Laura was sitting at her desk at work beginning to worry that she would run into week two and find Lynn Fine lying by Lake Ravine. Laura was about to make a call to Graveyard Hotel to see if there were any leads to the bomb threat and see if she can get a suspect. The phone rang and Laura picked up the phone.

Laura: Hello Detective Dunim.

Sara Novella: Hi I know this may sound strange. My name is Sara Novella and I live in upstate New York. I am calling because I think I may have some information relating to Lynn Fine's kidnapping. I went on Mr. Fine's book signing events in NY, Maryland and New Jersey. There was someone following him and it led to a bomb scare. I reported a strange guy making comments and threats to Mr. Fine and his family. He was making threatening comments about Mr. Fine's daughter. He was also harassing other fans and I saw security throw him out at three book signing events. The one in NYC at LC was a bit strange and I started getting suspicious.

Laura: Stop right there. Can I have your name and number again.

Sara: Yes. Sara Novella. 555-1212.

Laura: Thank you Sara. I was at LC book signing in NYC.

Sara: You were?

Laura: Yes. I was attacked.

Sara: Was it by the same guy. This guy kept saying bitch to Mr. Fine in the audience. He was really creepy looking. He had a weird looking eye, which made me nervous.

Laura: Yes! That was him a bit of a creep. I almost shot him.

Sara: My cousin took many photos of him and recorded him on many events. I was wondering if the department was interested in photos.

Laura: Yes! Thank you so much for calling. Mr. Fine was very very very concerned about you and he mentioned you to me. Send me those photos.

Sara: He did? I honestly didn't think he cared.

Laura: He was very concerned. I was just going to call the hotel to get your number and give you a buzz up. We must have esp. Can you fax me those pictures?? Or send them through me email? @ lauradonimlapd.com.

Sara: Sure. Also, too I have a name. We thought his his name was Roy. At the Convention Center in Maryland he was room 230, I think! Or 666 Graveyard Theater. Not Sure. I finally realized he was on the same floor next to us at Graveyard. He kept taking the elevator to the sixth floor. So maybe he was the sixth floor. I would double check that. Creepy!

Laura: Omg! Thank you so very much a great lead. I would like you to fly out to Los Angeles to testify and see if when we catch him and bring him out here.

Sara: That would be kind of difficult? Hotels are very very

expensive and I don't know anyone out in Los Angeles.

Laura: Well you know me. I work at Hotel Chiller. How about I book you compliments of the Hotel free for two weeks until we catch this guy.

Sara: I don't know. I don't know if I can get off from work that many days. I do have several days. I would need a note or call to my boss if you decided you really needed me.

Laura: How about I call your boss and tell him what a terrific person you are.

Sara: Well I do security at work. He would be thrilled to hear that.

Laura: If they give you a hard time you will have a job with Mr. Fine out here.

Sara: WOW! I doubt they will.

Laura: Okay. I will call your boss. Give me Your work number. (Sara gives her number over the phone). Then I want you to get on the next plane to Los Angeles Airport and if you need financial help, I will cover the costs. You call me back. Our department will help you.

Sara: Um.

Laura: What is it Sara. Speak fast.

Sara: I am disabled and what if something happens and I'm in danger.

Laura: Well. I can speak to the judge and Mr. Fine. I'm sure Mr. Fine will help you out. But I doubt you have anything to worry about. But if something does happen, we will help you. You keep me informed if something happens and give me your medical information. We can alert the hotel as well.

Sara: Are you going to tell Mr. Fine I called.

Laura: Yes, I am. But not right this second. I want to call Graveyard Theater and see if I can get a phone number and address. Then a warrant. So, I need to hang up and you get on the next plane. I will inform your boss. Do Not worry.

Sara: Okay. I will look up air fare.

Laura: Let me know when you are booked and leave me a message with your work information as well. I will book you a room with a two week stay, complimentary breakfast and dinner at the hotel for two weeks. Not sure what else Mr. Fine will give you but I'm sure he will be very very thrilled with this lead you provided.

Sara: Okay Laura I will see you in two days. Were You that blonde that was by Mr. Fine at LC in NYC?

Laura: Yes. Yes, I was.

Sara: Oh!! I saw you looking at that guy when he was making remarks. You handed out the copies.

Laura: Yes. Yes. That was me. Okay. So, I will see you my friend in two days. Do you have family or kids to tell that you have to leave?

Sara: (Sara clammed up).

Laura: Sara are you there?

Sara: No, I don't really have family, just a couple of cousins, and no one to tell. But as soon as I get off the phone, I will book airfare.

Laura: Okay, sounds like a deal. Talk to you later.

They both hang up the phone and Laura calls Graveyard Theater. Hi my name is Laura Dunim can I speak to the person in charge of this hotel?

Tammy 2: Answers the phone. The person in charge is not here tonight. How can I help?

Laura: My name is Laura Dunim. I work with the Los Angeles Police Department.

I am looking for a person who was acting suspicious your hotel when celebrities stayed for the autograph signing event. You had the author Richard Fine who is wonderful staying with you. He was being harassed by a guy named Roy. I just received a suspicious phone call that he was on the second floor 290 or 666 and harassing fans.

Tammy 2: Yes. I know who you are talking about. I was getting calls on him a few days that one Saturday by security guards. He was crazy.

Laura: Am I allowed to get his name from you. Can you pull up his name? He is under suspicion for Lynn Fine's kidnapping.

Tammy 2: Well. I cannot give you his name on my work time cause of confidentiality reasons.

But I get off of work in three minutes. I can call you back because I do know his name and I can give it to you then without even researching on the computer. In the meantime, I can look up his address and print it out. No one has to know. We have to do it anyway for clients and pull up their records on all floors to check. (The other manager tugs Tammy on the side).

Hold on Laura. I have to place you on hold

Tammy 2: Places Laura on hold. (looks at the manager) What is it?

Manager: If it's in connection with a crime you can give their names and address. Maybe he had something to do with the bomb threat. So, I would give it to the detective. I have your back.

That guy was a Moron.

Tammy 2*:* Thank you. I wanted to do that for Mr. Fine. He is so very nice and doesn't deserve this.

Manager: You're welcome.

Tammy 2: Hi Laura. Thanks for holding. I just asked my other manager and she said to go ahead and give you his name and address. So, I will do that now. As a matter of speaking I think I can give you his address. Tammy pulls up the weekend

of the autograph show. Goes to Room 666 and the name Roy Dell comes up from Los Angeles, California.

His name is Roy Dell. Lake Ravine Apartments 2F Tally ho Drive, Los Angeles California. 999- 999-9999 is the phone number.

Laura: Omg! Thank you so much Tammy.

Tammy 2: You're Welcome! Will you tell Mr. and Mrs. Fine I was asking for them and I hope their daughter returns home safely? They were so nice and gracious to me. They gave me their autograph at the desk. They told me I had the same name as the other receptionist in Maryland and wanted to remember me. Mr. Fine nicknamed me Tammy 2 to remember my name. They said they came across Tammy and Angels. He autographed a picture for me Tammy 2. I also gave them a percentage off.

Laura: I will. I just wrote down your name. I'm sure he will be calling you and saying thank you.

I will be calling your manager at a later date and letting them know what a great worker you are. You should be working for Mr. Fine.

Tammy 2: I would love to come work for him.

Laura: Well I will put in a word for you. There are always openings for loyal fans who lookout for one another. Thank you again Tammy. Talk to you later.

Tammy 2: I hope you catch him.

Laura: Well now we will. Have a Great Day.

Chapter 21

The Confession

The Laura hangs up and walks over to Detective Briggs office.

Laura: Briggs you busy?

Briggs: Looks up. Now I am. But I charge $5.00 for ten minutes of your time.

Laura: Very Funny. I charge $20.00 for every minute of anyone's time. Especially when I come up with a lead to a kidnapping case.

Briggs: Ouch! Now that's interesting as he is eating a chocolate cream donut and drinking coffee. Want a donut?

Laura: No Thank you.

Briggs: Bring it on. You have that look.

Laura: I received a tip from Sara Novella.

Briggs: The girl that Mr. Fine was suspicious of.

Laura: Yes. She sent me photos of a guy stalking Mr. and Mrs. Fine. He was making threatening comments about their daughter. He was going to harass Mr. Fine and do some stuff to Mrs. Fine.

Briggs: Really!

Laura: Yes. So, what I did was I had a name and I called the Graveyard Hotel. Sara said he was in room 666 at Graveyard Theater. The receptionist gave me a name and address and guess what?

Briggs: What?

Laura: His name is Roy Dell and he lives at Lake Ravine apartments in LA. I have his number and address.

Briggs: I want an APB brought on him ASAP! Bring him in. No actually, let's go to his place and get him.

Laura: Yes. You want to do it?

Briggs: Sure. It was your tip.

Laura: We work together.

Briggs called the officers to put an APB out on Roy Dell and bring him in for questioning. In addition, he called up the judge and asked for a search warrant to search the premises of Roy Dell's apartment and complex for any information regarding Lynn Fine's kidnapping.

Briggs sent over four officers to the apartment complex as he left with Laura in his car to head toward the apartment complex. Four Police cars and four officers pulled up to the front of the apartment building. Detective Briggs and Dunim pulled up as well. Two officers got out of their car and shielded themselves.

They opened the passenger door and driver's door. They kneeled down and pointed their firearms at the door. Two other officers assisted Briggs and Dunim as they entered to the front door and knocked on Roy's door.

Briggs: (Knocking) as he turns to the officers and Laura. Shush. He puts his index finger over his mouth. He mumbles to Laura. I have an idea. I hear someone.

Briggs: UPS guy.

Laura: Laughs.

Briggs: Shush. And he smirks.

The two officers are smirking too. Roy comes to the door. He opens the door and tries to shut it real fast.

Briggs: Not so fast buddy as he holds the door open. Roy tries to go for a gun but

Briggs throws him to the floor.

Laura: Steps in with the officers and the pull their guns out.

Briggs: Flips Roy over. He puts his left arm behind his back. SURPRISE! It's over Roy Dell.

Where is Lynn Fine where is she?

Roy: I don't know!

Briggs: We are coming with a search warrant. Where is Lynn? Did You Take Her?

Roy: No, I don't have Lynn Fine. I was hired to stalk them by another person.

Briggs: Who who did it?

Roy: That guy or actor.

Briggs: Which actor? Which actor are you talking about?

Roy: The one from Riker's Hospital. The one who attacked The Fines in the eighties. He wanted their daughter away from the Fines to get to know her. He was planning on killing Mr. Fine. He hired me to stalk Mr. Fine and plant evidence on his property.

Briggs: You have a number and address. Do you know where he is keeping her?

Roy: I'm not sure. A house A condemned house off of Lake Ravine. He's not going to kill her though. I know she's still alive.

Meanwhile, Laura is going through Roy's stuff. The wall had pictures of Mr. Fine and Mrs. Fine with their fans at all the book signing events with slash marks. There was one picture of Mrs. Fine by herself with lipstick all over her lips saying pretty bitch. She opened up a file draw and saw a ton of crazy photos with knife slits in them with Mr. Fine's photo. She also pulled out photos of Mrs. Fine with knife slits and kiss marks. She pulled out Roy Martin's number.

Laura: Sick! Is this it? She also pulled out whiteboard that stated how to kill Mr. Fine and Mrs. Fine. Were you planning on killing the both of them?

Roy: I wasn't I was just thinking about it and keeping Mrs. Fine for myself.

Laura: Sick? Arrest him Briggs. We have more than we need.

Briggs: Tell us where Roy Martin is and we will put in a good word for you.

No one will be getting Mrs. Fine except Mr. Fine. Laura walked into the bathroom which was pretty large.

Roy: Martin is keeping Lynn in a condemned yellow stone stucco house. It sits on a mile acre of land about twenty minutes from Lake Ravine. It's 666 Tavern Road, Los Angeles. There are twelve pine trees on the property with a small lake to the right and a farm market on the left.

The yellow stone stucco house looks fine in the front with two windows and slate for stairs. There are two high steps. In the back there is a deck. But the deck is decapitated and green. All the back doors are boarded up. The front doors are boarded up as well. It looks like no one lives there. Roy has a Black Van. You get get downstairs through the side and there are a set of double doors and concrete steps that goes downwards. That leads into the basement up to the foyer and kitchen. Make a right and go upstairs. Lynn is on the large bedroom on the left. She is chained to the bed and when go over, she is usually gagged an cannot yell. He ties them, then he drugs victims and ties them with rope. Then he suffocates them. Lynn is still alive.

He's not planning on killing Lynn Fine. He is just holding her captive until he captures Mrs. Fine. He did four kidnappings and three murders. He kidnapped and murdered the other girls to frame Mr. Fine. He was going to start to frame him next week. He was going to leave some of Lynn's stuff on Mr. Fine's property and call the police department. He wanted me to frame Mr. Fine.

Briggs: Is that why you were on it a while back??

Roy: Yes. But Mr. Fine came out and I took off.

Laura: Were you the one who call Mrs. Fine from NYC and stalked me in the bathroom with pretty bitch?

Roy: Yes, it was me.

Laura: You're under arrest. So, I suggest you come clean if you want a lighter sentence. Come clean now. Did you kill anyone?

Roy: No. I just helped with the kidnapping in Lynn Fine.

Laura: Do you know where Roy Martin is right now?

Roy: I don't know. Maybe with Lynn.

Laura: Can you call him?

Roy: Maybe. He is expecting a call from me today in regards to the update on items I left at Mr. Fine's house. He wants me to plant more of Lynn's items on his property.

Laura: Well, why don't we give him a buzz. You help us catch Lynn Fine. Maybe we can pull a stunt and get you off with harassing charges and say you went undercover to help put Roy Martin away. You may not have to do any time whatsoever. Did you call in the bomb threat to Graveyard??

Roy: No. It was Roy Martin. I thought about it but I decided not to go through with it. Roy Martin did it. I was getting kicked out of autograph rooms too many times.

Laura: Okay. When will you be calling Roy Martin?

Roy: In about an hour. Can you tell the cops' cars to get off the property? If he comes here, I don't want him to see cops' cars he will run.

Laura: I will call of the cops' cars and I will tell cops to stay and remove their cars.

Laura calls the cops and tells them to remove the cars.

Roy: Fair enough. I will help out.

Laura: Okay. I am going to tap your phone. Briggs do we have a tap in our car?

Briggs: As a matter of speaking I do. I forgot to take it out.

Laura: Okay go get it. Let's tap the phone. Were you afraid Roy Martin was going to turn on you?

Roy Dell: Yes. Yes, I was. I saw the look in his face and felt that he was just using me to keep a low-key cause he just got out of the psych ward. I also overheard him say that in the house where he was holding Lynn. I could take you to her. She is alive. She is okay. She's a pain in the ass. Man, she is tough. She's the first victim to escape three times and get caught.

Laura: Well she's defending herself. Okay. Thank goodness he's not planning on killing her.

Roy Dell: No. He's keeping her alive. I have to bring her dinner this afternoon. He's going to let me know where to pick up dinner.

Laura: Detective Briggs and I are going to be hiding in the back seat of your car when you deliver dinner to Roy.

Briggs: Okay. The phone tap is hooked up but if he calls from your cell can you put it on speaker. So, when he calls everything will record and we can get information on him that he has Lynn Fine.

Roy Dell: Yes. I will put my speaker phone on. I do it all the time and he knows that. He should be calling in thirty minutes.

Laura: Should I call Mr. Fine and Let him know we have leads on his daughter and she's at least alive?

Briggs: I think so. At least they will know she's coming home.

Laura: Okay.

Chapter 22

Is Lynn Safe?

Mr. Fine, Mrs. Fine and Whisky are in the kitchen. Mrs. Fine is cooking dinner and Whisky is watching Mrs. Fine cook and looking to eat. Mrs. Fine is making Chicken Cacciatore. The tomato sauce was coming to a boil and Mrs. Fine was stirring the onions, mushrooms, peppers and chicken thighs & legs.

She started cutting up the Italian bread and took out the butter. Whisky was walking in between and around Mrs. Fine's legs eating crumbs off the floor. Whisky went to Mr. Fine. Mr. Fine bent down and picked up Whisky to put him on his lap. He gently petted him under the chin and on top of his head as Whisky playfully licked Mr. Fine while wagging his tale.

Mr. Fine: (spoke to Whisky as Whisky was licking him) Stop eating my ties.

Then the phone rings. Mr. Fine puts down Whisky and the dog sit by his legs.

Mr. Fine: Hello! Mr. Fine speaking.

Laura: Hi Mr. Fine it's Laura. I have some excellent news! Is your wife there?

Mr. Fine: Yes. Yes, she is. Hold on Laura. I will put you on speaker phone

.**Laura:** Okay. Are you both on?

Mr. and Mrs. Fine: Yes, we are.

Laura: One of your fans Sara Novella called my office today. She came forward and was very honest about what happened at Graveyard Theater. She had a bit of a conscience. She reported a suspect to our office. His name is Roy Dell.

Roy was deliberately harassing you. He wanted to frame you for Lynn's kidnapping. I say kidnapping because we are 100% SURE LYNN IS ALIVE AND WELL. Mr. and Mrs. Fine were yelling and Whisky was barking with excitement when he saw the Fine's happy. Scotch even came in and barked as well with all the excitement. Mr. Fine hugged Mrs. Fine as Mrs. Fine began crying.

Laura: Mrs. Fine are you okay?

Mrs. Fine: I am fine.

Laura: Sara then gave us the name of the room number Roy Dell was in and we were able to apprehend him. Roy fearing for his life, decided to come clean. There are two people involved in Lynn's kidnapping. Roy said Roy Martin from Riker's Hospital is responsible and has her hostage. In addition, your buddy Tammy2, from Graveyard Hotel provided us with Roy's address and phone number. We are at Roy's apartment right now. Roy has agreed to help us bring your daughter home.

Mr. Fine: He has?

Laura: Yes. His charges will be lowered if Lynn is alive and well.

Mr. Fine: Even though he is a creep for what he did to us, we won't bring charges against him. We want Roy Martin!! He's been and harassing my wife for years.

Laura: Well you can let the judge know that when he goes before the judge.

Mr. Fine: I will. How's Sara?

Laura: Sara will fly out tomorrow to California. I just got a text. She is staying at Hotel Chiller.

Mr. Fine: She can also stay with us as well. We will take Sara in.

Laura: I will ask her what she wants to do. She's financially strapped and may need to do that.

Mr. Fine: I want to talk to Roy.

Laura: I would recommend not to. We will bring Lynn to your house at around 7pm. Roy Martin has no clue we are coming in for him and he will be in for a surprise of his life. I would recommend staying put until we go in and get Lynn. I don't know what condition Lynn will be in.

If she is hurt, we will bring her to a hospital and I will text you once we have her. I am going to have a few police cars helping us out. I am also going to have an ambulance on standby as well coming. We have plenty of back up and resources to get Lynn to safety. We will bring her home by 7pm.

Mr. Fine: I think she should go to the hospital first for and be checked out. We can meet you over there.

Laura: Well let's see first. I think she would want you and Leena first.

Mr. Fine: You're probably right. See how she is.

Okay we will be on standby.

Laura: Okay. See you in a bit. Roy Martin from Riker's Hospital has about an hour of freedom left.

Laura: Turns to Briggs. You ready?

Briggs: Let's get this idiot once and for all!

Roy Dell: The phone rings. Earlier than I planned! He goes to Briggs and warns him.

Briggs: Answer it. Let it ring twice and put it on speaker.

Roy Dell: Takes his cell phone out of his pocket and puts it on. He points to the cell phone. Roy puts the speaker phone on.

Roy: Hello Martin, what's happening?

Roy Martin: What time can you be at the house?

Roy Dell: What time do you want me?

Roy Martin: In about an hour. Can you pick up two pizza pies from Mike's Pizza on Lake Ravine road and get me three pies? I told Lynn if she behaved that I would get her pizza. I should kill her now like I did the other three and drop her off by the lake. I still may if I get pissed off enough. She thinks I'm keeping her here in the house for another week but I'm not sure, what will happen after that. I assure you, if she escapes one more time, I am getting my gun and shooting her to kill on the spot. So, this may be her last supper. One more time she escapes, she's dead.

Roy Dell: Made a face. Oh. I thought you were keeping Lynn.

Roy Martin: Well I was planning on it but she keeps getting lose and running away. Someone may find her here. I don't know how long I can hold her in this house. So, I will think about that tomorrow.

Roy Dell: Okay. I will get two or three pies. Then what?

Martin: Bring them around to the left side of the house and I will leave it unlocked. Blow your whistle to let me know you're here. (both hang up the phone).

Briggs: (Laughed). Then said, we will see you gets shot!

Laura: (Shut up she says quietly and puts her index finger over her mouth but is laughing). Laura knew Briggs was nuts; and they would be going under cover and delivering pizza to Martin.

Roy Martin: Turns to Laura and Briggs. Pizza should be ready in thirty minutes.

Briggs: Are there any cameras in that house?

Roy: There are two cameras by the left side of the door?

Briggs: Damn. What if you distract him for several minutes? Leave the side door open and we could get in? Then his eyes are off the camera.

Roy Dell: What about giving us about fifteen minutes to start putting the pizza down. Those cameras aren't the best cameras. They pick up movement. Many times, Roy thinks its animals. So, he really won't be looking for you. I will tell him there were three dears outside by the side door basement.

Roy: He will also probably be tying Lynn up so his eyes will be off the cameras when we come to the side door. I think it will be okay that you show up to the side door. He will be by Lynn's bedroom making sure she doesn't get away.

Briggs: Sounds like a plan. Alright all Let's do this!

Everyone was on their way to get pizza and Lynn. We can have pizza for dinner after this is over on Roy Martin. (Laura laughed).

Chapter 23

Does Lynn Live?

Meanwhile, back at Martins house, Lynn Fine was in one of the rooms. She was locked in her room from the outside. She heard Martin coming up the stairs. Martin was coming up the stairs with a bandana to gag her so she didn't scream and rope to keep her tied until Roy came with the pizza. Martin opened up the door.

Lynn fought to get out and tried to push her way through Roy. Roy grabbed both arms.

Roy: Again! You will not get away from me and he slaps her in the face. She falls to the floor. He grabs her left arm and puts it behind her back sitting on her bottom. He grabs her right arm to tie both arms together. He picks her up and drags her to the bed and sits her on the bed. Then he ties her to the bed.

Lynn is almost crying but won't give into tears which was pissing Martin off.

Martin: Your pizza is coming so I suggest you be quiet. If you're not quiet I will kill you.

Understand? UNDERSTAND? As he screams in a maniac voice. He leaves and locks the door from the outside.

After Lynn is tied, she realizes Martin didn't tie her enough. So, she unraveled her hands and was able to get her hands free. It took about fifteen minutes to get the knots untied.

Lynn: Come on she said, as she struggled to untie herself. Lynn was free.

Lynn went to the door to listen to see if Martin was outside. She peaked through the keyhole and saw no one was there. Lynn went through the draws in the bathroom. She remembered Roy left the nail file in the draw. She knew Martin was away from the door and looking out for pizza. Lynn found a nail file and grabbed it.

Lynn then walked over to the door and played around with the lock with the nail file. The door unclicked. Lynn opened it quietly. She then grabbed her coat and a few things to fight with to hide in her pocket. She grabbed the large can of spray hid it in her pants. She walked out the room for the first time into the other room directly across from her room.

She went into the room. She looked on the right wall. One wall had pictures of her mother and father with knife cuts from the book signings. It says: Kill Mr. Fine underneath. The whiteboard was hung up underneath as well. It was stating ways to kill Mr. Fine and frame Mr. Fine Mr. Fine.

She looked to the left wall. She saw a picture of the victims murdered in Lake Ravine. The first picture she saw was a picture of Susan Stone and information. There is also a clipping of new stories on her disappearance. Underneath, Susan Stone there was a lock of her hair.

Then she goes to the next victim Denise Morris and there was a picture of her, with a lock of her hair. There is a new story clipping and her necklace by her neck underneath her picture. Last, she sees the third victim: Marie Rays with her lock of hair. There was also a news clipping underneath her all red heads she thought. She saw the perfume bottles on the dresser with the laced drugs next to it. She saw two guns. She grabbed one gun. She turns to the back wall and sees her picture. It's says keep Lynn and marry Mrs. Fine. Or, kill Lynn and marry Mrs. Fine. Will decided in two days. Lynn new she was next and needed to get out of there. She put her hands over her mouth and gasped for air. She kneeled over and cried for a second, feeling dizzy. She passed out for a second and got up.

Lynn forgot she left the door open to her bedroom. She walked back across and quietly locked her door from the outside. She set up the bed as if she fell asleep to trick Martin. She figured Roy Martin would be back and when he realizes she's missing this will distract him. Then, she can quietly go downstairs to the basement to the double doors to try to escape. She also knew she would be safer and be able to defend herself now with stuff available to her. She also knew the double doors would be open as well and she could run out. Martin always left the doors opened an hour after he got food from Roy. Lynn locked the door from the outside and hid out in the room by the living room to go downstairs. She peaked one more time to see if Martin was downstairs but he was not.

Lynn went downstairs one more time and hid in the closet. She was by the front doors. She took several deeps breath in the closet. She heard Martin coming up the stairs. Martin was on the second set of steps by the bedroom doors until he heard Roy come up with pizza.

Roy Dell: Comes in with two Pizzas. MARTIN YOU THERE AS HE SHOUTS? A HE MADE HIS WAY UP THE STAIRS.

Roy Martin: I'm here Roy. Roy comes back down the stairs and he tells Dell to put the pizza on the table.

Briggs and Laura quietly pull up in the driveway with two police cars and the ambulance. The police get out their vehicles. They open the doors of their cars and create a blockade with the doors. They get behind the passenger's door and driver's door. They bend down behind it.

Briggs and Laura get out. Briggs puts his index finger over his mouth to the officers and signals to the officers be quiet. The officers were laughing as Briggs and Laura were sneaking in.

They get down with their guns out. Briggs tells the officers he and Laura will go in first and he needs two more officers. The other two can stay behind. Briggs and Laura with the officer walk to the left side of the house by the double basement doors. The doors are open. They quietly walk down the cemented rectangular stairs and up the basement stairs with the two officers.

Briggs: Puts his index finger over his mouth too tell all to be quiet.

Martin: Did you hear something?

Roy Dell: I didn't. But I saw three dear outside. My phone went off. It was vibrating.

Martin: Maybe it was that. I heard something earlier too. I will grab two plates and forks let's get Lynn some pizza. Martin takes three slices of pizza and puts it on the plate. Here you carry this because I have to open up Lynn's room and untie her.

Roy: Okay give me the plate. Roy and Martin go up the stairs. They are on the second set of stairs.

Lynn: Quietly opened up the closet door. Briggs opens up the basement door and sees Lynn. He puts his hand over his mouth. He says come here with his index finger, realizing Lynn escaped. He hands Lynn to the officer's downstairs.

Officers: quietly asked her where's Martin?

Lynn: He is upstairs to the left unlocking the bedroom. He's going to flip when he realizes I am missing.

Briggs: Get out of her. There are two cops' cars outside.

Lynn: Okay. He's nuts and he has a gun on him and in the other room. He also has fake perfume bottles and drugs.

Briggs: Okay. Thanks. I already know about it.

Two police officers escort Lynn to safety outside.

Briggs: Let's go Laura. They quietly creep up the first set of stairs. Briggs and Laura take out their guns.

Meanwhile back at Lynn's Room Martin made his way to Lynn's Room to untie her. He is about to open the door.

Roy Martin: Okay Dell, I got the key Let me open up the room. Roy begins to open up the room with the key. He opens the door. Dell puts the pizza down. Martin goes over to the bed to wake Lynn up thinking she's sleeping and finds Lynn missing.

BITCH! GOD DAMN IT! **GOD DAMN IT!** She's dead this time. This is the last time she is going to pull this charade with me and leave. BITCH BITCH BITCH. I am killing her. Go find her Dell. You look Up here I will go downstairs. When I get her, she is dead. Where is my gun?? Roy Dell goes to the left and Roy Martin goes to the right. Roy went into the next room to grab his gun. Roy took out his gun. Martin walked out of the room with his gun in his hand. I'm coming to shoot you Lynn. Roy Martin runs into Briggs.

Briggs: (Holding his weapon and hears Martin). Freeze Police. Briggs points the gun to Martin.

Roy: Is still moving.

Laura: (Laura has her gun out). Freeze police I will shoot!

Roy Martin: Roy puts his hands up but reaches for his inside of his jacket.

Briggs: (Shot him in the leg). Roy fell to the floor holding his leg in pain screaming like a maniac. Briggs went over and roughly cuffed him quickly until the medical team got there.

Laura arrested Roy Dell. Lynn hears the gun shot from upstairs as she is sitting by the ambulance with a blanket on her. She was fine and was bleeding from the side of the head but didn't realize it. The medical technician was wiping the blood and cleaning up the bruise on her head.

Briggs and Laura bring out both Dells in handcuffs as one dell went into the ambulance and one Dell went into the officer's cars.

What do you think will happen next? Will Lynn go to the hospital or does she go home? Are there more victims? What does Sara Do? Does Sara stay with The Fines? What does Mr. And Mrs. Fine Do? Stay tuned for book two.

Thank You

To all my family members.

To my parents:
William and Madeline Vespe who told me never to give up on my writing. To my brothers, sisters, nieces and nephews for supporting my book

To My Aunts and Uncles: This book is also in loving memory of Anthony Enrico who recently passed a few weeks ago.

To Roland and Josephine Tudisco who help me in hardships and when I became ill.

To all my cousins, friends and Facebook friends: I love you dearly and you always stand by me whatever I say.

Photographs were of Scotch and Whisky were done by Mia Murphy. Thank you so much. Their real names are Wookie Murphy (Whisky) and Gizmo Murphy. (Scotch).

To Mia and Joseph Murphy & Teresa and Robert Tudisco:

A Big Thank you for taking me on celebrity book signing events when I was sick and too sick to do it myself. Thank you to my cousin Mia Murphy for keeping us safe during the bomb scare events in Parsippany, New Jersey. It was cold, windy and rainy that day.

To The St. Augustine's Parish And Catholic Daughters Of America:

Thank you for all your support when times were hard. Thank you for your prayers when I became ill. Thank you. Father for the call when my car nearly flipped over in the last snow storm of 2018. Thank You to The Catholic Daughters of America for their ongoing concern with my medical issues and never leaving me alone with the doctors.

SPECIAL DEDICATION & THANK YOU!

A special Thank you To Robert Wagner & Stefanie Powers for their true caring of fans during hard times and Crisis. Before this bomb scare event happened about an hour before I was speaking with Robert Wagner and Stefanie Powers during A Photo Shoot. They were making sure I was okay. Thank You Robert Wagner and for coming back after the bomb scare threat and all the chaos; saying goodbye to fans. It was gracious of you to be truly concerned. It's a story that needs to be shared with everyone. It was still a wonderful weekend and God Bless Them for their care of Fans. I left the hotel knowing I was cared for by two great people. What an experience it is to spend the weekend with Robert Wagner and Stefanie Powers.

* This story is based on the television series Hart to Hart which appeared in 1980 and true events that occurred during an autograph signing show of Robert Wagner and Stefanie Powers.

*This story is based on events that occurred in Parsippany New Jersey during an autograph signing show event on the weekend of October 28th, 2018. This book is dedicated to staff, security and law enforcement officials who responded so bravely during a bomb scare threat at the in Parsippany NJ during an autograph signing show. Also, to all Celebrities, venders and fans who attended this festival a huge thank you. For copyright purposes I could not print real names and places.

The real story is as can be found under bomb scare threat:

Bomb scare, gas leak chase 3,000 from Chiller Theatre Fest...

www.freep.com:0/story/news/2018/10/28/bomb-scare...
Bomb scare chases 3,000 from Chiller Theatre Fest at Parsippany NJ ... police were advised by a front-desk employee at the hotel that an unknown suspect had just phoned in a bomb threat.

At about 2:30 An immediate evacuation of the HOTEL was conducted after a report of a gas leak. During the evacuation, the Parsippany Police Department's Communication Center received a phone call from an employee at the Hilton Hotel front desk. The employee reported that an unknown suspect had just phoned in a bomb threat to them. An immediate evacuation of the entire structure was ordered, along with a request for mutual aid due to the number of guests present. The Morris County Sheriff's Office K-9 Unit and Bomb Squad responded to the scene, along with members of the New Jersey State Police K-9 Unit. A check of the interior and exterior of the structure was completed and no devices were located In Parsippany NJ. Guests were allowed back in the hotel at about 6:30 pm.

Pictures of Photos that were done before, during and after the bomb scare events at Chiller Fest in Parsipanny, New Jersey.

This Photo was Taken about an hour *before* the Bomb Scare Threat

Pictures of Photos that were done before, during and after the bomb scare events at Chiller Fest in Parsipanny, New Jersey.

This photo was taken right before the fire alarm went off. We were still inside and just about to pay. The fire alarm went off. We were still inside the room and evacuated together.

Pictures of Photos that were done before, during and after the bomb scare events at Chiller Fest in Parsipanny, New Jersey.

This photo was taken during the Bomb Scare Event.

This photo was taken the following day.

About The Author

Jane Vespe was born on October 16, 1967. She was raised in Highland, New York which is located in the Hudson Valley New York. Jane Vespe grew up watching television shows from the seventies and eighties. After High School, Jane went to college and got her Master's Degree in Science in Education. She took many courses in English and writing as well.

In February 2014 Jane as in a bad automobile accident and pulled from a car crash. Within several months, she had a double spinal fusion. The double spinal fusion was in November 2014. When Jane woke up the day after her surgery one morning she couldn't breathe well and knew she caught pneumonia. Jane caught pneumonia. As a result, was hospitalized for weeks and recovery was hard.

While recuperating Jane dreamed about travelling to the stars. She tried to contact celebs when she was in the hospital. Jane was transferred from one hospital in the Hudson Valley to a rehabilitation center to continue recuperating. For weeks she was breathing through an oxygen tube and walking with a walker. Recuperation seemed to take forever. Her fever was very high every day until about the first week in December of 2014.

In December of 2014, Jane was released from rehabilitation and started on a slow road to recovery.

In May, 2015, Jane was doing much better and was released from therapy, walking normally. It was recommended to go to the pool and swim which did for two years. In October 2016, Jane saw celebrities doing book signing events and travelled to see the stars for two years after. In addition, she attended weight loss meetings and took off fifty pounds. Jane went on many autograph signing shows and dinner parties with celebrities. This is how *Hotel Chiller* Began.